TV IN THE HEAD

KEVIN TAO MOHS

First American edition published in 2016 by Lucky Bat Books

ISBN-10: 1943588279

ISBN-13: 978-1943588275

Cover design by Nuno Moreira
Manufactured in the United States on acid-free paper

FIRST AMERICAN EDITION

Mohs, Kevin Tao
TV in the Head

About the Author

KEVIN TAO MOHS is a cable television executive who has worked at National Geographic Channel, Discovery Channel, Animal Planet and TLC in various creative capacities. During his graduate studies in Radio, Television and Film at the University of Maryland, the writings of media theorist Marshall McLuhan captured Mohs' imagination. McLuhan posited that all media are extensions of our human senses, bodies and minds. The idea of media and mind and body being one inspired Mohs to write a screenplay entitled EYEtv for his graduate thesis. In that farcical tale, the inhabitants of a far off planet have small television devices implanted in their heads soon after birth. The idea seemed far-fetched decades ago, but as media technology evolved over the years, the notion of televisions one day being in our heads didn't seem that ridiculous to Mohs, so he decided to revisit his story and place it on earth in the very near future.

As a television producer and cable executive, Mohs has firsthand knowledge of the power of the media and has collaborated on such successful series and specials as The *Story of God* with Morgan Freeman, *River Monsters*, *Dragons: A Fantasy Made Real*, *Deadliest Catch*, *Life Below Zero*, and *Gold Rush: Alaska*.

Mohs has consulted on two books for young readers (*Dragons: A Fantasy Made Real* and *The Most Extreme*—inspired from the television series he created). He has also published another work of fiction entitled *The Devil's Bite*.

Mohs lives in Maryland outside Washington DC with his wife, two kids and various pets. He's hard at work on his next story.

ALSO BY KEVIN TAO MOHS

The Devil's Bite

Dedication

To all the parents locked in a battle with electronic devices for their children's attention. May direct human interaction always be the ultimate victor. And to Yihung, Tienne and Sean for their continued love and support.

One

GIL HAD BEEN casing the house in the Capitol Hill neighborhood for over an hour waiting for the occupants to go to bed. He saw where they kept the stash and noticed a window opened slightly in the kitchen. That would be his way in. Despite the typical steamy night in Washington, D.C., Gil shivered. He couldn't control the thoughts in his head. They hit him all at once and he had difficulty processing them.

I'm hungry. I should eat something. I should've killed dad the first time he hit mom. What's that noise? Am I being followed? Vince stole my shirt last night. I'm gonna get him. Please make this stop.

All he wanted was to be numb again. He didn't want to think about the terrible things that happened in the past or the fact that he didn't know where his next meal would come from or where he would sleep. He wanted to be swallowed by nothingness. He had been told that if he succeeded, he'd get his bliss back. He could put his worries to rest and live in the now.

The lights downstairs switched off. Gil saw the silhouettes of two people walking up the stairs to the second floor. He crept out of his hiding place in the bushes in the backyard. Soon it would be time. Soon he'd get the relief he'd been promised. He needed to wait just a bit longer.

There, the lights in the bedroom were off. Time to go.

* * *

The AC was broken again. Mark Wilson cursed to himself for not having the old system replaced when they moved into the house. The bedroom was stuffy and no breeze came through the open windows. He lay on top of the blankets, tossing and turning, trying to get comfortable in the stifling heat. His wife lay fast asleep next to him. She was blessed with the ability to fall asleep as soon as her head hit the pillow. Mark stared at the ceiling and let out a frustrated puff of air. This was going to be a long night.

He heard a sudden crash. It sounded like a dish or cup dropping in the kitchen. Mark looked at the foot of the bed and saw the cat. Someone or something was in the house.

Mark tried to find the nightstand in the darkness. As he searched the surface, he hit the lamp, but caught it before it fell. He slid his hand across the top and down the side until he found the drawer handle. Pulling it open, he located a small metal box. Inside were electronic chips about the size of a postage stamp. He found the one he wanted and pressed his finger next to a slot on the left side of his head behind his eye socket, which ejected another chip. He replaced it with the new one.

His vision changed. He could see in the dark and his hearing was heightened.

His wife mumbled, "Honey, what are you doing?"

"Someone's downstairs," he said. "I'm going to check it out. Stay here and call the police."

She closed her eyes, as if deep in thought, then opened them again. "Okay, they're on their way. They said to find a place to hide until they come. Just send down the personal drone to check it out. "

Mark heard footsteps on the stairs. "I left it in the briefcase downstairs," he whispered. "No time to wait. Someone is coming up here now. Go in the closet."

He searched the room for some sort of weapon. His heart was about to beat out of his chest. He had to get control of his breathing and his nerves.

*　*　*

Gil's mind raced. He told himself to stay focused. He knew what had to be done to get the relief that had been promised him. If it meant killing someone, so be it. But there were so many distractions, so many things to think about. He realized he had body odor. He hadn't noticed that before. How long had he stunk so badly? Was that why he had lost his job? No, it was because his boss was evil. That's right, the man had it in for him. Wait, why was he in this house? He forgot for a moment. Then it came back to him. Gotta go upstairs. He had seen Wilson carrying around that box. It must be in the bedroom. He needed to make the switch.

He heard a noise at the top of the stairs. Someone was there. He looked up just in time to see a hammer swinging towards his head. Then a pain like he'd never felt before crashed down on his forehead. His skull cracked open, followed by fuzzy dancing lights. In a flash, all his worries were gone. The lights in his head faded and he drifted into a deep nothingness.

Two

AN ELECTRICAL CORD connected Marshal McClure's head to the console in front of him as his sleek black SUV silently made its way through the darkened streets. There wasn't a visible steering mechanism, just glowing instruments and gauges that displayed information on speed, engine functions and directions.

McClure was a broad shouldered man in his early thirties with close-cropped black hair, warm brown eyes and a Mediterranean complexion inherited from his mother's side. He'd never served in the military, but his rigid and serious demeanor made the impression he had. His partner in the passenger seat, Ed Goodwin, on the other hand, looked like a disheveled bureaucrat with pasty white skin who rarely left his desk. He was overweight with a loose fitting suit, dusted with dandruff flakes from his oily hair. Goodwin's gaze was unfocused as they rushed along the DC streets.

"We'll be there in five minutes," said McClure.

No reaction from Goodwin.

Irritated, McClure continued. "You have the camera and forensic equipment? I think there's more to this case than a simple breaking and entering."

No response.

"Do you have the entertainment chip in? You know regulations. You have to use the work chip on duty. Not only is using the entertainment chip on duty against regulations, it's against the freakin'

4

law. Get with it, man." He slapped Goodwin upside the head.

Goodwin shuddered as if being woken up from a deep sleep. "What, what?"

McClure pointed to the narrow one-inch slot on the side of his head. "Change the chip."

"Can't a guy get a break? I'm just sitting in the car. What else is there to do?"

McClure shook his head in frustration. "A man broke into the house of the chief lobbyist for the Personal Vision Corporation and got his head smashed. I have a feeling there's more to this case than a simple breaking and entering."

Goodwin sighed as he ejected the chip from the slot behind his left eye. He reached into his pocket and pulled out a case with different colored chips. He grabbed the gray one and slid it into the slot.

"Special Agent Goodwin reporting for duty," he said with a sarcastic sneer. "Hey, how come you don't use the wireless device to drive the car? I'm the old guy here. I thought you younger guys jumped at the new gadgets."

"I don't trust the wireless version. Remember that big pile up last week on the Beltway that killed a mother and four kids? Turns out her car picked up the signal from someone else's device and steered her van right into the path of an oncoming truck. There was nothing she could do to regain control."

"Leave it to you to always look on the sunny side of things," said Goodwin. He snorted. "God, I really want to put that entertainment chip back in. I was in the middle of a really great sex scene. Cut me some slack. You've seen my wife. Let me have this little fantasy."

"On your own time," said McClure.

Two years earlier, McClure left the Washington Metropolitan Police Department. He had risen quickly in the force and made detective at 27. His rise created some jealousy and resentment among his fellow officers and when he left for the more lucrative private sector, the resentment increased tenfold.

He now worked for the Vision Enforcement Agency, also known as the VEA, the enforcement and investigative division of the vast and powerful Personal Vision Corporation. It had an exclusive contract with the US government to pursue any crimes associated with the device and to enforce any regulations regarding their transmission and usage of the Personal Entertainment Devices (PEDs).

In the company's pioneering days, the devices were surgically implanted in adults only. But as they grew in popularity and the surgeries became more routine, they became an option for parents to consider for their children soon after birth. The devices were carefully connected to the optic nerve and auditory canal so sounds and images went directly into the brain.

The Personal Vision Corporation quickly grew in power and wealth, destroying all competition. Soon it owned all the channels and became a monopoly. It controlled the messages being sent right into the heads of the captive audience and negotiated lucrative deals with advertisers and entertainment companies. It convinced government officials that it could monitor itself. Thus the VEA was created. This secretive service shut down pirate channels, took addicts nicknamed PEDheads off the street and investigated accidents and crimes associated with the usage of the devices. They were a busy operation.

The SUV quietly pulled up to the curb in front of the home on Capitol Hill. McClure noticed a couple of police cars. He shook his head in disgust as he caught sight of square jawed Sgt. Bryce standing in front of one of the vehicles.

"Here we go," he said under his breath.

Bryce caught sight of McClure and walked over to him. "What's the Boy Wonder doing at a breaking and entering case? Isn't this below your pay grade?"

"Good to see you too, Bryce. Where's the body?"

Bryce stepped in between McClure and the home, blocking his path. "You never told me why VEA men are here. This is our case. We can handle it all on our own."

"This is the home of one of our executives, so this will be a joint investigation. If you have a problem with it, take it up with my superiors."

Bryce sized McClure up, as if trying to determine if this was a bluff. He stepped aside with an exaggerated gesture and motioned for McClure to pass. "Have at it, Boy Wonder. But the body stays with us."

As McClure stepped into the entryway, he saw the victim crumpled on the landing with blood trailing down the steps. He tapped Goodwin on the arm. "Get some images."

Goodwin took a pen-sized cylinder from his pocket and pointed it at the corpse. He pressed a button on the side as he captured various angles. "Can you believe soon they will be coming out with a camera that goes right into your eye? No more transmitting images from the camera to the chip. I won't have to lug this thing around anymore."

"Plus, you won't lose it as often," said McClure as he noticed Mark Wilson and his wife sitting on a couch. Both appeared shaken, but neither said a word to each other.

"Goodwin, get some close-ups. I'm going to ask the Wilsons a few questions."

The Wilsons' gaze didn't move as McClure sat on the stool in front of them. He coughed to get their attention, but they didn't respond. "Mr. and Mrs. Wilson, I'm special agent McClure from the VEA. I have a few questions for you."

No answer.

McClure pulled out a controller from his holster. He aimed at the Wilsons and pressed a button. They both gasped as if awaking from a trance.

Irritated, Mrs. Wilson spoke first. "What are you doing? I'm talking with my family, letting them know I was okay. You've cut me off."

"Sorry, Mrs. Wilson, I just have a few questions and then I'll let you back to your communications. I know this must've been terrifying."

Mark Wilson looked at McClure's badge to make sure he got his name. "Agent McClure, let's make this really quick. The would-be burglar is dead and I'd like to move on."

"Did he say anything to you? Did he make any demands?"

They both shook their heads. Both were extremely fidgety, like antsy children.

"Agent McClure," Mrs. Wilson said, "I'd like to get back to my messaging. This is making me uncomfortable." She stood up and began pacing the room while wringing her hands. "I can't stand the silence. Please turn the PED back on."

Mr. Wilson put a firm hand on McClure's arm. "I can hold on a bit longer, but I don't think she can. She rarely switches her PED off. This is too much of a shock to her system."

"Enough, enough, enough," said Mrs. Wilson as her agitation increased. She clenched her fists as if enduring a great pain. McClure pointed the controller at her and pressed a button. She gasped in relief and her entire body relaxed. Her eyes glazed over.

"Thank you for that," said Mr. Wilson. "I can answer about one more question and then I really need to get back in my head. I was in the middle of a tour of Tahiti and I want to get back there. Good for the soul in such dark times."

Before McClure could continue with the questioning he noticed Goodwin in the hallway signaling for him to come. "Pardon me. I'll be right back."

As McClure walked past him, Mr. Wilson eased back into his chair, stared off into space and returned to the sunbathed shores of Tahiti.

"You should really take a look at this," Goodwin said and pointed to the victim's fractured head. "The skull is damaged from blunt force, but there's something really strange about the slot for the PED. Something is jammed in there as if the chip melted inside."

McClure bent down and took a close look at the side of the skull. He sniffed around it and detected the odor of melted plastic and metal. "We should take this back to headquarters."

"Take what?" asked Bryce who suddenly appeared in the doorway below. "You aren't taking the body anywhere. Like I said, this is our jurisdiction, Boy Wonder."

"Look at you," McClure said and sneered. "Keep acting like this and someone might mistake you for an actual cop. I didn't realize you knew big words like *jurisdiction*."

With a furrowed brow, Bryce shook his head. "Funny, you've got five minutes before someone from the medical examiner's office picks it up." He walked back toward his cruiser.

Goodwin gave McClure a worried look. "You heard him. You're not taking the body."

"Of course not, give me the micro bone saw."

Goodwin reached into his bag and pulled out a small device consisting of a handle and an inch long blade. McClure grabbed it and pushed a button on it, springing the blade to life. He knelt next to the body and pressed the saw into the skull next to the PED slot. A fine dust of bone particles flew up around the blade and Goodwin almost gagged from the burning smell. McClure cut a rectangular shape around the PED slot. He used his fingers to press into one side, causing the other to stick out. Then he pulled out a nice, neat chunk of skull.

"Got what I needed. Let's go."

* * *

From an alleyway across the street, a man shrouded in shadow watched the police at the household. He cursed himself for entrusting such an important mission to an unstable addict like Gil. He knew his boss would be upset, but he usually figured a way out of trouble and he would do it again. It was time to start the next mission. The target he'd been following would be in a vulnerable location soon, so he needed to move. As a backup, he noted the slovenly VEA agent that pulled up to the crime scene with his partner. He could prove useful to him. He made a mental note to pay him a visit later.

Three

THE ONLY SOUNDS on the crowded dance floor were the shuffling of shoes and the panting of people exerting themselves as they moved to a beat only they heard inside their heads. The darkened room with pools of light was a surreal scene. The twenty-something strangers made no attempts to mingle.

Even though Elizabeth Jenkins was now a young adult, this was her first time on a dance floor. It took all of her courage to venture through the doors of the Grave Club. She'd heard of this new fad where people all gather in one room, tuned to the same music channel and moved to the rhythm. It seemed like an odd thing to do for enjoyment. Every form of entertainment was already supplied through the PED. Why leave the comfort of your own home? But an unexplainable urge had come over her recently and, for some reason, she wanted to be near other people. With her shoulder-length blonde hair and peach complexion, she stood out in the crowd, but no one took any notice.

Elizabeth grew up in the PED age, so she never knew a different life. Before her time, students used to assemble in buildings called schools where they obtained knowledge and interacted socially. From what she saw on the old programs like *Saved by the Bell* and *Welcome Back Kotter*, it could have been enjoyable. Instead of having to walk or drive to a building, she simply inserted her educational chip. The chip served as a receiver and transmitter for all the classwork she needed.

For many years that was enough for her, but something seemed to be missing. She couldn't put her finger on it. Those people in those ancient programs didn't have all the blessings that came with the PED, but they appeared to have something else. The way they placed a hand on a friend's shoulder or slapped someone on the back reinforced some sort of connection. They seemed to need each other and they sought companionship. It really didn't make sense, but she felt drawn to it.

That's what brought her to the Grave Club. A sign next to the entrance declared that she was entering a personal drone-free area. Once inside the club, a digital display on the wall listed the channel to tune into and, before she knew it, her mind was flooded with a pounding rhythmic beat and vibrant swirling colors. Without even thinking, her body moved to the music. She didn't resist. She lost herself to it, moving, almost as one, with the hundred or so bodies in the club, all of them sharing the same experience at the same time.

Elizabeth was absorbed in her own world, but she also felt a connection to others. With all the bodies in the room, the temperature was rising. Someone's sweat soaked arm rubbed against hers. At first, she was disgusted by contact with the perspiring bodies, but she eventually gave into the experience and became one with the room.

As the crowd moved in their collective trance, she saw a tennis ball-sized drone fly into the room. It hovered over the center and then emitted a bright flash of light. The dancers covered their eyes and then fell to the ground, writhing in pain. The screeching in Elizabeth's brain was unbearable. She tried to change the channel to tune it out, but it persisted. No matter what she thought or did, the sound intensified as her mind filled with a bright, brutal light.

She saw two disheveled individuals enter the room, stepping over the bodies in the doorway. One looked nervously around. He was clearly having difficulty focusing and was a bit lost.

The second guy walked up behind the first guy and hit his arm. "We've got a job to do. Let's move. Once this is done, you'll have what he promised."

The first gave him a toothless smile. "Yes, yes. I can't take this much longer. I need it."

The two approached Elizabeth.

The second guy used a dry calloused finger to release her chip. She could feel his hot breath on the side of her face and it reeked like sour milk. She struggled to control her gag reflex, then everything went dark and quiet in Elizabeth's mind. He inserted a new chip and Elizabeth felt a burning pain. Before she could cry out, it was gone. She heard, "All done."

The first guy quickly removed chips from the other club-goers and replaced them with new ones. As he did so, Elizabeth saw sparks emanating from the devices, followed by a puff of smoke. The second guy gave the first guy a thumbs up. "Let's get the hell out of here."

The second guy patted her shoulder and winked at her. Without a word, the two men left the club. Elizabeth thought of 911 to call for help, but no signal went through. She couldn't connect with emergency dispatch. The chip they had inserted into her head had severed the connection.

She rubbed the slot on the side of her head and felt a hardened ridge. The slot was sealed by something. Whatever was put into her head was not coming out. There was nothing in her mind—no music, no images, no messages, just her thoughts. She felt naked and vulnerable. She heard others around her moaning. Some of them screamed when they realized they were cut off from Personal Vision. The thought panicked her. Then something burst to life in her mind. It was the image of a man in a hood made of sackcloth. His face was hidden in the shadows.

The figure spoke in a raspy voice, "This is Brother Socratease. Don't worry, I'm not that stuffy Greek philosopher, Socratese. I am a free thinker, but a bit more twisted. Just do as I say and I promise you relief."

Four

PERSONAL DRONES BUZZED around the National Mall like swarms of gnats transmitting aerial views to the tourists sitting on the conveyer belts below that transported them from one site to the next. A few of the drones trailed alongside McClure as he jogged alongside the Vietnam Memorial. He was used to being a curiosity to the tourists who had rarely, if ever, seen a real person physically exerting himself. His morning activity often drew strange looks from people comfortably taking in the sights from the moving sidewalk. Walking long distances and running had gone out of style ages ago, but McClure was an old fashioned guy, clinging to a ritual he had seen in old television shows. From what he observed in those classic programs while in the Academy, cops actually had to pass physical fitness tests. Now the testing was about using and manipulating technology. Thanks to the controllers, the need to chase down perpetrators and forcefully subdue them no longer existed.

McClure's friends and family couldn't understand why he insisted on physically exerting himself, but it made him feel better. It cleared his mind and refreshed his muscles. He felt more in control. He only tuned into the audio programs while jogging. The music gave him an extra boost of energy and enhanced the experience for him.

As he passed the Lincoln Memorial, he glanced over at the crowd that had stepped off the moving walkway and now stood at the base of the steps that led up to the giant seated figure of Lincoln that seemed to gaze down upon them like Zeus from his perch on Mt. Olympus.

He noticed a few children in the crowd and he wondered whether or not they were naturally conceived or created in the lab. So few people had kids naturally these days. The interest in sex had decreased over the decades with the rise of Personal Vision. With the vivid pornography channels, all the sexual stimulation now happened within the mind. No one needed to risk physical encounters with others. As a result, the childbirth rate decreased radically and the need for creating babies in the laboratory rose. The population was thinning out. Soon, the family as McClure knew it would disappear. He feared everyone would be too self-absorbed to care about others.

He shook his head to clear away those thoughts. He was an employee of the Personal Vision Corporation and he knew, if used properly, that Personal Vision could better society. Still, what he saw at the crime scene last night nagged at him. Was it a random breaking and entering by a PEDhead or something more? He left the section of the skull that he had cut out at the lab. The technicians would be showing up for work soon and he hoped they could tell him what was fused inside the slot.

As he neared the Martin Luther King monument on the tidal basin, he received a message from headquarters. "Agent McClure, report to the lab immediately. You'll be interested in what we've discovered."

Five

THE REAL WORLD was quieter than Elizabeth had imagined. The cars whispered up and down the street. A few early morning risers strolled or took the moving walkway without exchanging words. No one made eye contact with anyone else. They just moved from place to place totally absorbed by the myriad of entertainment options playing in their heads.

For the first time in her life, Elizabeth felt different from everyone else. It was as if everyone had been invited to a party except her. The quiet gnawed at her. All her life her mind was filled with sights and sounds fed by Personal Vision. Depending on the chip she placed in the PED, she could watch movies, play games, travel to exotic locations or send messages to friends and family. The lack of constant distraction unnerved her. The world around her was more vivid than she had ever noticed before. As she turned the corner, the rising sun caught her face. She shielded her eyes from the glare with her hand until a shadow moved over her. Looking up, she noticed an orange hued sky filled with white clouds that looked like cotton balls. If she looked closely enough, the outline of one of the clouds looked like a witch's head with a pointed hat and a hooked nose. Elizabeth never had a reason to gaze at the sky before. Sure, she had glanced quickly in the past to see if rain or snow was on the way, but to just look up for no reason was new.

She still longed for the escape into the world of Personal Vision, but the panic she had felt earlier in the club subsided. The man with the hood had told her to get out of there quickly, so she sneaked out before any cops arrived on the scene. Since then, the signal from Socratease had gone dead. All that was left in her mind were her thoughts and the pain from the burn on the side of her head. Instinctively, Elizabeth rubbed the thin scab that covered the PED slot. She wondered what the hooded figure wanted. She walked around the city in the early morning hours trying to sort it all out, but she found no answers. She just wanted to get home, shower off and fall asleep.

Finally, she spotted her apartment building. Relief was only steps away. Sleep would be such a great escape. After some rest, she could figure out a solution. If anyone could help her, her dad could. As President and CEO of Personal Vision Corporation, he had the resources necessary to repair the damage done to her PED. With the infected chip fusing the slot completely closed, she knew this was more complicated than her local technician could handle. As she stepped into the lobby, Elizabeth was taken aback by the sterile surroundings. The walls were white with no artwork to adorn them. It was a plain, empty room. She had walked through this lobby countless times before but never really paid attention to it until now. She guessed the landlord must've decided it wasn't necessary since no one really appreciated their surroundings anyhow.

Just then the hooded figure appeared in her mind. Elizabeth gasped. "This is Brother Socratease. Until you do as I ask, I will be the only channel you have access to. I know you are probably going through withdrawals and desperately wanting that mind numbing escape known as Personal Vision. If so, the relief will come, I promise you."

The words sent shivers through Elizabeth's body.

A stranger was now occupying her mind. "What do you want?" she asked out loud.

There was no reply.

She looked around the room for a place to hide, but she realized she had nowhere to go.

"I can't read minds, so I don't know what you're thinking right now, but I imagine you're scared and confused," Socratease said. "Unfortunately, my chip is rather rudimentary and only has a one way messaging service unlike Personal Vision. But you can receive my signal and that's what matters. I need you to get close to your father. I've left something in your apartment that you can give him. If you don't do what I say, I can make life miserable for you. I can send signals that will drop you to your knees and make you want to open up your skull. I will give you a small dose right now."

Elizabeth's mind filled with a high pitched sound and blinding strobe lights. She leaned against a wall to steady herself. The sensation was overwhelming and agonizing. Seconds seemed like minutes. Her head felt as if it were going to explode. Then, it stopped. She slid to the ground, exhausted.

"Now, get the gift I left in your apartment and arrange to meet with your father today." Then he was gone.

Six

THE PERSONAL VISION headquarters building on Pennsylvania Avenue was enormous. It dwarfed the Department of Justice building nearby. Elizabeth had been there many times, but this was the first time she really noticed its size. In it were studios where entertainment, news and dramatic programs were produced. There were also rooms where gaming geniuses devised new programs that fed directly into the brains of their customers.

The advertising department was the most profitable division. The ads were pretty simple, really. They consisted of subliminal messages imbedded within programs that urged viewers to purchase a product or service. Viewers wanted things without even realizing it. When consumer groups tried to persuade Congress to prohibit this form of advertising, the Personal Vision Corporation flexed its considerable muscle and squashed any proposed legislation before a bill could even make it to subcommittee. Personal Vision promised to self-regulate to ensure the power was not abused. Public furor died down and was forgotten as the populace was lulled by the myriad of offerings provided.

After passing through security, Elizabeth gazed at the giant murals that decorated the walls of the massive marbled gallery. Like the Stations of the Cross she'd seen in Catholic Churches, they told a story. In this case, it was the "Enlightenment of Humankind." Painted in the style of Michelangelo's work in the Sistine Chapel, the first image portrayed the Greek god Prometheus giving fire to humans. The next showed those same humans gathering around a fire they had made. At the center of the painting was an elderly man with an animated face pointing a finger and telling a story to others.

Each painting progressed through time, depicting various stages of human development, forms of entertainment and dispersion of knowledge. One painting showed a crowd gathered in a medieval town square enjoying a performance of the *Punch and Judy* puppet show. Another portrayed a Rockwellian scene of a clean-cut family sitting in front of a giant radio, listening to their favorite drama. In each scene, the technology progressed and eventually included television sets, hand held tablets, video game consoles, Google glasses, 3D visors and finally Personal Vision. In the final image, a male figure stood tall and heroic. No longer was he dependent on something external for his information and entertainment. The power resided within him. Humankind was now empowered.

These giant paintings hung silently in the grand, empty hallway. Elizabeth heard no sounds but her own footsteps on the marbled floor. The paintings were originally created to awe all who visited this place of power, but no one looked at them anymore. They were too distracted by the sights and sounds inside their heads. Elizabeth had never noticed their beauty before or taken the time to contemplate their meaning. To her, they had just been some sort of decorations not worth looking at whenever she visited.

Seeing the last painting of the man with the PED slit on the side of his head, reminded her of why she was there. Absently, she rubbed her right hand on the bandage covering her scab. She wondered if she really could do what Socratease had demanded. She realized that even though she had lived with her father for most of her life, she didn't really know him. She couldn't recall the last time they'd had a long conversation. What would she say or do when she got to his office? She no longer had messages, music or entertainment programs to occupy her time and mind. She was on her own now. It would take effort to figure out how to interact with someone else, especially her father.

* * *

McClure walked past the corpses in the morgue. The scene was morbid, but the music in his head was light and upbeat. He was on duty and had to use the chip for work with its limited entertainment options.

The morgue was a top-secret operation in the basement of the headquarters, where bodies of people killed in PED-related incidents were brought for examination. Technicians and medical experts examined the bodies and the devices. People died for a variety of reasons. Sometimes PEDs were improperly inserted in unsterile conditions, leading to an infection in the brain. Surges of stimulation sometimes burst blood vessels in the brain and caused fatal or crippling aneurisms. Most of the deaths were from accidents caused by distracted people.

As a police officer, McClure had seen the gruesome aftermaths of these accidents, but one incident was seared into his memory more than any other. One winter night as a young officer, he received a call to rush to the scene of a domestic dispute. He was the first to arrive at the townhouse. He could hear the hysterical shrieks of a woman inside. It sounded as if she were screaming "What have you done?" over and over again. McClure tried the door handle, but it was locked. He pounded on the door and yelled, "Police, open up," but all he heard were more screams.

Per his training, he kicked the door just below the knob to break the lock, but it didn't give. He kicked again and it still held firm. He had no time to wait for back up to arrive with a breaching ram. Being one of the first officers with a prototype of Personal Vision inserted into his head, McClure sent a message back to headquarters letting the dispatcher know that he was going in.

The large front window was his best way in. He jumped down from the front stoop, searched the area for anything to break the glass and found nothing. Back then, police officers still used guns, so he pulled his pistol out and pointed it towards the floor as he fired so he wouldn't hit anyone in the room. A spider web of cracks exploded from the hole. McClure pulled his hand into his jacket sleeve for protection and broke the weakened glass. He created an opening big enough for him to climb through, careful not to cut himself on the jagged edges.

"This is the police," he shouted. "Come out to where I can see you with your hands up."

He stopped to listen, but he heard nothing but the sound of the refrigerator engine cycling. Then he heard a *thump, thump* as if a heavy wet sack were being dragged up wooden stairs.

"Come down here now. I have back up right outside."

Thump, thump.

The only light in the room came from the dimly lit streetlight outside. As his eyes adjusted, he could make out the corners of the room. It was mostly bare except for a few oversized stuffed animals and a dollhouse in one corner. There were kids in the house. He bolted out of the room and toward the thumping sound. As he entered a hallway, he could barely make out a trail of blood from the entryway down the hall and towards the stairs.

McClure held the gun out in front of him, ready for an attack from any side. He moved with deliberate caution to the base of the stairs and looked up in time to see a door close with a loud slam.

As he dashed up the stairs, his feet slipped slightly on the still wet blood. He caught himself on the railing with his free hand. When he reached the top, he stood to the side of the door, carefully reached for the handle and turned the knob. The door wasn't locked. He pushed it open, peered inside and gasped at the horrible sight.

* * *

When Elizabeth entered her father's office, she wasn't sure what to do. Now that she lived on her own, she only saw him when she visited her old home to check on her mother's condition. When she was young, it was always her mother who had held her when she needed comfort. Her father was uncomfortable with human contact. Now that her mother had slid into a catatonic state, the old house seemed empty and she had a hard time building up the courage to visit. Whenever she did, Elizabeth distracted herself by jumping between the various entertainment options in her head. She was there in body only, much like her mother.

Even though she probably hadn't seen her father in a month, he looked older than she remembered. There was more grey in his thinning hair than she recalled and his increased weight slowed his movements. Francis Jenkins had once been an energetic and driven man, but the man she saw in front of her was just a ghost of who he had once been. He stood from behind his desk and took a few steps toward her while awkwardly reaching out an arm, unsure what to do with it.

"Elizabeth, I didn't expect to see you here," he said with a confused look.

She fiddled inside her jacket pocket with the device Socratease had left for her. If she acted quickly, this could all be over. She remembered the intense pain that filled her head earlier and shivered at the thought.

"I, I am worried about mom," she said unconvincingly.

Her father gave her a quizzical look and pointed at her head. "What happened to you?"

Covering her bandage with her free hand, Elizabeth said, "I wasn't paying attention where I was walking and a tree branch scratched the side of my head. Lucky I didn't poke out my eye."

This is the time to strike, she thought to herself, but she hesitated. What would happen to her father if she did what she was told? Would she kill or cripple him?

Her father raised his hand in a signal for her to stay put. "Sorry, someone is sending me a message."

He paced back and forth for a few moments, then looked at Elizabeth in astonishment. "Do you have something to tell me?"

Something had gone terribly wrong.

"I'm going to send you a message and an image," he said. "Take a look at it and then tell me what's going on." He squinted his eyes in concentration. "Got it?"

Elizabeth could no longer receive any signals other than those from Socratease. If she didn't say anything, her father would know something was seriously wrong.

"I'm not using a chip right now. I had to get it out before a scab formed over it from that scratch. What's wrong?"

Her father gave her a distrustful look as he pushed a button on his desk, prompting a thin clear screen to rise up from the center. Soon a still image filled the screen. It was Elizabeth dancing in the club. In the still frame, she could see herself with her eyes closed with a slight smile on her face. This was clearly before the attack.

"Yes, I went out dancing," she said. "I know it looks weird, but it's starting to catch on."

"That's not what concerns me. What happens next is what I want to know more about." Her father's gaze moved from her to something behind her.

As Elizabeth turned to look, she saw a large security guard walking in the door. He stopped right behind her and stood silently at attention.

"Watch," her father said, drawing her attention back.

A video began to play and cut from various angles. As the masses moved almost in unison to a silent beat, two figures walked into the room. They looked around and then one of them pointed to Elizabeth. Then, suddenly there was a flash and the video feed went out.

"I don't think that scratch came from a tree branch. What happened after those men saw you?"

Elizabeth eyed the floor nervously. The security guard blocked the only way out. "Maybe they were pointing to someone behind me. I don't know. I don't remember those guys."

Her father moved closer to her. "Elizabeth, I know something must've happened. I've gotten reports that there was an attack at the club. The culprits paralyzed everyone and substituted their chips with corrupted ones that fused into their PEDs, making them inoperable. I want to take a look at your PED. We can help."

As he reached for her, she panicked. She pulled out the controller device from her pocket and pressed the button. Simultaneously, her father and the security guard grabbed their heads in agony and then fell to their knees.

Elizabeth pulled out a chip from her pocket with her other hand and held it up in front of her. Socratease had ordered her to replace her father's chip with this one. He promised that, afterward, her torment would end.

She pressed her finger against the slot on the side of his head. The chip slid out. Her father looked up at her with pleading eyes and managed to murmur, "No," through the pain. He had always been distant, but never mean or cruel. It was just the way society was nowadays. She really couldn't blame him. She paused for a moment. Putting the chip in would be so easy, but she didn't know what would happen to him. She didn't want to kill or maim her father.

She felt a hand grab her leg. Spinning around, she noticed the guard on the floor, clutching her leg. It took all his might to overcome the painful signal being sent into his mind. The grip was loose, but it startled her and she dropped the chip. She ran out of the room.

Seven

AS MCCLURE STOOD amongst the bodies in the morgue, the memories of that night when he was a young cop flooded back. When he entered the bedroom, the first thing he saw was a giant crucifix painted with blood on the wall. On the bed below were three bodies. A boy who appeared to be about five was on one side, a girl around two on the other and, in the middle, a woman in her late twenties. All three were in their pajamas and had their throats slit. The woman was positioned with her arms outstretched on either side with the kids placed on her arms facing toward her as if she were holding them in a death embrace.

At the foot of the bed stood a dark-haired man covered in blood and holding a large kitchen knife. He slowly turned his gaze from the bed towards McClure. His eyes were red from tears.

"I released the demons that were in them. They're now at peace."

The man stepped forward and McClure raised his gun. "Drop the weapon."

The man dropped the knife and it clattered on the wooden floor. He seemed to be in a complete daze and didn't resist being handcuffed. When McClure brought him back to the station for booking, he was surprised when his superiors told him not to put the case into the system. Instead of being jailed, the suspect was turned over to VEA agents. McClure was told this fell under their jurisdiction.

He argued at first, saying it was a murder case and had nothing to do with the Personal Vision system, but it was of no use. He was furious, but also intrigued. That's when he knew being a cop wasn't enough. He wanted to get into the big league, to deal with the tougher cases. He wanted to be a VEA agent.

A hand on his shoulder jolted him into the present, back to the morgue. He spun around and saw a short, dark-haired man in a lab coat. Jerry Orvieto was a nervous guy, but McClure couldn't deny his genius. So many medical examiners were lazy corporate hacks who reported whatever they thought VEA wanted to hear, but not Orvieto. He was genuinely curious and often worked through the night to find the cause of death. His findings didn't often sit well with his superiors, but that didn't matter to Orvieto.

"It took you long enough to get here," Orvieto said. "I wanted to share what I found before putting it in my report. Go to channel 525. I sent you something that I extracted from the damaged PED you brought in last night."

Channel 525 was McClure's secure line for receiving and transmitting reports and materials. He pictured it in his mind and found the file with the case number. He saw the pictures from the crime scene that his partner had taken. Nothing unusual there.

"What am I looking for?" he asked.

Orvieto fidgeted anxiously next to him. "Look for the skull fragment. Once you're in there, move towards the melted chip. I was able to find remnants of a signal. The chip wasn't made by us. Someone is manufacturing their own pirated chips that corrupt the PEDs and only allow one channel. And it's a channel I've never seen before."

McClure focused his mind, found the fragment, the melted chip and then mentally dived deeper. He saw mostly darkness, but there was a light in the distance. He strained harder to get closer. The light flickered, but an image became clear. It was a hooded figure with a faint voice. "This is Socratease. Do as I say and you will be free."

"Who is Socratease?" asked McClure.

Orvieto shook his head. "Never heard of him until last night. Yours was the first damaged PED, but more came in. The victims are still alive and at the clinic. They were attacked at a club by two men who replaced their entertainment chips with the bootleg one. All of them are reporting a loss of connection to the Personal Vision network and the appearance of the hooded figure who calls himself Socratease."

McClure stared at the man in the hood and tried to make out a face, but it was obscured by the hood's shadow. When he tried to increase the resolution, the image just got fuzzier. What did the man want?

He heard an alarm from channel 111, which was reserved for top emergencies within the HQ building. He switched from 525 to 111 where the head of security was talking to the camera.

"There is an intruder in the building." A still image of a young woman appeared. McClure recognized her as Elizabeth Jenkins, the CEO's daughter. "She was last seen fleeing the executive offices and going towards the lobby. Secure all exits. She is to be apprehended and not killed."

McClure bolted out the door, his adrenaline pumping.

* * *

Elizabeth was out of breath. She couldn't even remember the last time she ran. Dancing the previous night was the most exercise she'd had in years. She felt lost. A cold, hard emptiness hit her. She was on the run from her father with no idea where to go. She stood in the lobby, desperately trying to catch her breath, when she noticed a familiar figure walking rapidly towards her. It was the man from the club. The one with the smelly breath. He was coming for her with a determined look.

"Did you do it?" he asked urgently.

She shook her head no.

With disgust, he spit on the floor and grabbed her arm. "It was a simple job. When I tell Socratease, you're going to suffer."

"Don't tell him. I can try again," she said.

She heard footsteps echoing in the giant lobby. She turned her attention from the man with the smelly breath to see a VEA agent rushing towards them with his controller raised in front of him.

The intruder taunted the agent. "Go ahead, give it a shot."

"Both of you, raise your hands above your head," the agent said.

"If not, will you push that button?" the intruder taunted.

Elizabeth watched the agent push the button and felt nothing. Puzzled, the agent glanced down at the controller to see if it was on. He raised it again and pressed the button. Nothing.

Before the agent could react, the intruder was right in front of him, coming with a right hook that connected with the side of his head. The agent stumbled sideways from the blow.

Before the intruder could land another one, the agent launched himself into his midsection, shoving a shoulder hard into his abdomen.

It knocked the breath out of the intruder, but he didn't collapse. He raised his elbow and thrust it hard into the middle of the agent's back. Elizabeth could see the pain on his face. She felt compelled to help him, but this was the best time to get away. As the battle raged, she edged her way quietly toward the doorway.

If she didn't move quickly the lobby would be filled with more security officers. As the door opened, she glanced back one last time to see the agent motionless on the ground with the large, foul breathed intruder standing triumphantly over him. She wanted to rush to his aid, but it was time to go. To where, she didn't know.

Eight

ELIZABETH PUSHED HER way through the thick brush, trying to find a clearing to rest. She had worked her way to Rock Creek Park near the National Zoo where the stream valley carved a rugged and natural oasis in the midst of a heavily urbanized area. She had visited the zoo when she was younger, but had never ventured into the woods that surrounded it. She felt safe tucked away in bushes as if the world she knew was far away. She figured there would be no cameras in the woods so they couldn't follow her movements. The streets were filled with cameras secured to buildings, light posts and even drones hovering overhead. Almost everyone wore a portable snap-on camera on their body.

The branches scratched her, but she pressed on until she found a small opening and a pile of dry leaves to rest on. She sat, caught her breath and looked at the canopy overhead. Above her was a giant sycamore tree with leaves larger than her hands. A gentle breeze created a comforting, rustling noise among the dancing branches. The earthy scent of decomposing leaves combined with the sweet aroma of honeysuckle blossoms reached her nose. Something tickled her hands that were pressed down on the ground next to her. As she peered down, she noticed tiny ants crawling on her. She brushed them off, almost without a second thought.

She was being stimulated by things outside of her, not by messages generating within her brain. It was liberating and scary at the same time. She felt engaged with her surroundings, but she couldn't escape into her mind for comfort.

She had no idea when Socratease would flood her mind with that terrible signal again, but she knew she had escaped for the moment. She was also getting hungry. The adrenaline that had been pumping since the previous night had disguised her growing hunger, but now it was in the forefront. She decided to rest until dark and then sneak back into the city.

* * *

The two blows to his head left McClure in excruciating pain. One punch had hit him on the side of the face and the other had landed at the base of his skull and knocked him out cold. He felt embarrassed for being beaten so easily. Most suspects lacked the coordination or muscle power to resist arrest, and the controller had proven useless against this suspect. The culprit was disconnected from the network.

When he opened his eyes, he realized he was no longer in the lobby. He was in the office of Francis Jenkins, the president and CEO of the Personal Vision Corporation.

"Glad to see you're going to make it," said Jenkins.

"I got caught off guard. It won't happen again," McClure said as his eyes adjusted to the brightly lit room.

Jenkins pulled up a seat next to the couch that McClure was sprawled on.

"What I am going to tell you stays between us," Jenkins said. "Do you understand?"

McClure sat up and nodded yes.

"That young woman is my daughter. Her mind has been poisoned by a person with criminal intent. I want her found before she falls into the hands of this man or before she's harmed in any way."

"Is this person named Socratease?" asked McClure.

Jenkins stared at him in stunned silence. He took in a deep breath as he decided what to say next. "I'm not sure how you know about him, but yes, he goes by that name."

"Then the guy in the lobby must work for him."

"That's my suspicion. His PED has been disabled, like the victims at the club last night. We can't track him, so we've tapped into the grid of cameras around the city to see if we can locate him that way. We need to find Elizabeth before he finds her."

The intensity faded in Jenkins' eyes as he said her name.

"Don't record this case in your files. What you're doing is a personal favor for me." He stood up and walked over to a cabinet and opened one of its doors. In it was a large safe. Jenkins pressed his finger to an electronic pad and the front of the safe slid open, revealing a helmet and a gun. "You'll need these."

McClure picked up the pistol like an old friend. Its weight and heft felt good in his hand. The need for guns had waned over the years with the rise of Personal Vision. In its place the controller was now employed as a nonviolent method used to subdue people. But McClure knew if he wanted to have any hope of bringing this suspect in, he would need to do it the old fashioned way. It was time to be a cop again.

Nine

TIM WEILAND STRUGGLED for breath. He felt his eyes bulge and his face flush as the foul breathed man pressed his forearm into his throat and pinned him against the wall.

He couldn't understand why asking for a spare temporary chip would enrage the stranger he'd seen hurrying down the street. He used to have a respectable life with a job before he became a PEDhead. Then, to escape his troubles, he spent hours upon hours enjoying entertainment programs and erotic brain stimulation until he stopped going to work altogether. Without employment, he couldn't keep up with his Personal Vision payments and his chip delivery discontinued. Without the chips, he couldn't access the programs.

Weiland finally took to a life on the streets begging for temporary chips so his mind could slip away to another place. These chips had a limited lifespan and were created for emergencies if you experienced a delay in shipments or had a faulty one.

Now he was fully in the moment as a very angry man held his fate in his hands. The assailant spoke through gritted teeth.

"I asked you, did you see anyone run by here? A young woman?"

Weiland shook his head no.

"You wouldn't lie to me, would you?"

Weiland felt his consciousness slipping. Soon he would be in permanent blackness. His breathing slowed. The assailant released him and he collapsed to the ground

"I would give up Personal Vision if I were you. It'll kill you if you're not careful."

* * *

Al kicked the PEDhead and walked away. He was angrier with himself than with the homeless man. Not only had Gil failed in his mission the night before, but now Elizabeth had slipped through his hands and he had lost her signal. He pulled out a personal drone from his pocket and tossed it up and down. It was the size of a golf ball with miniature camera lenses on all sides. He should have had it deployed when he entered the building.

The downside to being disconnected from the larger Personal Vision network was that he couldn't tap into the cameras located around the city. He could only rely on his personal drone for a video signal. He dreaded telling Socratease what had happened. He had hoped to have captured Elizabeth by now, but he wouldn't tell his boss before having one more look around the area. He opened the palm of his hand and the drone rose silently into the air. From inside his mind, Al was looking down at himself. His perspective rose higher and higher until he could see over buildings. The drone looked down Pennsylvania Avenue, back towards the Personal Vision Corporate Headquarters.

* * *

McClure sat in his car with his eyes closed as he scanned live video feeds from all over the city. He visualized the picture of Elizabeth taken by the security camera in the lobby and fed it into the stream of city scenes hoping for a match, but he came up empty. The security image had stamped the time in the lower-left corner. He rewound the feed to that time and played the video taken from the camera across the street from headquarters. After a few minutes, it showed Elizabeth bolting out the front entrance. She glanced to her right and then to her left and then darted in that direction.

Now he just needed to tap into a series of cameras in that general direction and see if he could piece together her path and capture her before Socratease and his henchman could get their hands on her.

Ten

DARKNESS AND EMPTINESS sent a shiver through Elizabeth's body. Day had given way to night and she was in an alien world. One where the only light she could see under the thick canopy of leaves came from fireflies dancing in the humid air. When she'd first spotted them, she dashed into the bushes, fearing they were drones searching for her. But when one landed on her arm, she realized it was only some form of living creature and not a mechanical, glowing sphere.

She wanted to reach out to a friend with her mind and send a message, just to be able to connect with someone, but there was only silence in her head. There were no signals coming or going.

She was succumbing to hunger and fear. Elizabeth wanted to scream for help, but the thought of that large man pursuing her kept her quiet. Tears poured down her cheeks as she sat on the moist earth and pulled her knees to her chin.

She hadn't felt so isolated since her PED was installed when she was very young. She'd been in her room when she heard her mother screaming in agony down the hall. When she pushed open the heavy door, she found her mother sprawled face down on the bedroom floor with her hands tightly clenched into fists. Elizabeth tugged on her, but her body remained motionless and her eyes open wide in a vacant stare.

Elizabeth was later told that her mother had suffered a stroke. The woman who had once surrounded her with love and warmth was gone. In her place was a shell kept alive through medicine and technology. Elizabeth's father had sworn that he would use his best scientists to bring her mother's mind back, but that was years ago and nothing had changed.

The growl in her stomach pulled her out of her thoughts. Hunger grew inside her and overtook her fear of the dark. She needed to get out of the park and find a food chew. The bite sized morsels were packed with flavor and much needed calories. But she feared that as soon as she stepped out of the park, cameras would capture her and alert her pursuer to her location. She would have to move quickly and rush back into the woods before he or her father arrived. Perhaps, with a food chew in her, she could collect her thoughts and figure a way out of this mess.

Elizabeth used roots and branches to pull herself out of the steep stream valley. When she reached the top, she peered out of the brush to the stores on the street bordering the woods. To the left she spotted a convenience store that advertised food chews.

People had lost interest in cooking and just wanted something that would satiate their hunger quickly with a pleasing flavor sensation. You could buy chews that contained all the flavors of various types of pizza, lasagna, salads, enchiladas—you name it. Most foods, themselves, only existed now in pictures and videos. Just consume a chew and your meal was complete. There was no time wasted preparing it or cleaning up afterwards.

Elizabeth took in a deep breath, working up the courage to run into the store, grab some bottles and escape before anyone could stop her. She had never stolen anything before, but she knew she would be tracked if she tried to charge it to her PED. Besides, with the damage to her PED, there was a good chance her internal charge card wouldn't work.

As she dashed into the road a piercing sensation jarred her brain. She collapsed to the ground in agony.

Eleven

THE ALERT WENT off in McClure's head. HQ had found a match. A camera picked up Elizabeth near P St. NW at the edge of Rock Creek Park. He assumed she must've been hiding in the park all day away from cameras. He pictured the location in his mind and the car glided quietly in that direction.

From what he could make out, she was crumpled in the middle of the street. McClure made a visual scan of the area surrounding her and saw no one, so she hadn't been immobilized with a controller. Someone farther away was sending a signal into her brain, probably the same person who had tried to abduct her at headquarters.

* * *

Al's personal drone beamed the video of the agent's car on the move. Al smiled to himself, knowing that the agent most likely had located Elizabeth. Al ran back to his car as the drone pursued the vehicle from above. He was determined not to let her get away this time. And he'd already tracked down the agent's slovenly partner.

* * *

Socratease spoke to her in a calming tone. "Elizabeth, wherever you are, I can make this pain stop. Just stay put and wait for Al to arrive. You are in control. All you have to do is not move."

Elizabeth forced her eyes to open. She didn't trust Socratease and needed to figure out a way to escape. Maybe she could catch the attention of a passerby. Through gritted teeth, she peered around her. She could see a clerk in the convenience store, but he was staring blankly in front of him, apparently absorbed with something playing in his mind.

With her brain throbbing to the beat of her heart, she continued to look for help. There was no one else in sight, but then she saw a grand church with spires. She just wanted to get out of the street and hide in some corner. She pulled herself toward the stairs in the front and painstakingly made her way to the door.

Once inside, she found a cavernous space with rows of pews and ornate artwork on the walls and altar. She had never been in a church before. From what she saw in the movies, people used to congregate in these buildings. There were channels now for your spiritual experience. You didn't even have to listen to someone preaching to you. Instead, you were flooded with light, warmth, soothing images and music.

"Elizabeth, Al will be there soon," Socratease said "Just wait for him."

She wondered if the man in her mind really knew where she was or if he was just blindly sending out a message to her. The pain in her mind made thinking difficult. To the side she noticed a structure covered in metal built into the wall. There were two doors on either side of it. She stumbled in that direction, her consciousness fading in and out.

She grasped a door handle and tugged on it. The door opened and she fell in. The door closed behind her. She was engulfed in darkness, but something had changed. The high-pitched sound and the pulsating feeling in her mind were gone. She couldn't hear or see Socratease anymore. The only sound was her own heavy breathing. She collapsed in relief, but only for a moment. Suddenly, she heard the echo of footsteps entering the church, followed by a man's voice yelling her name.

Twelve

THE LENS ON McClure's snap-on camera switched to night vision, boosting the levels of visible light in the seemingly empty church. He scanned for movement but saw none. He then adjusted the camera to FLIR so that any heat signatures in the room would show up in red or yellow.

Something caught his attention in the back of the church. He rewound the moment in his mind and saw it. A figure had quickly dashed through a doorway next to the altar.

"Elizabeth, this is Special Agent McClure your father sent me," he said calmly as he made his way slowly toward the door with his gun at the ready. "It's okay. He doesn't blame you for what happened. He knows that a man calling himself Socratease has corrupted your PED and is making you do things you don't want to do. Come with me and we can make the pain go away."

McClure edged himself next to the doorway. He detached the camera from his head and held it out so he could see around the corner. The heat signature showed a figure crouched in the corner. He couldn't make out if the figure was holding a weapon, so he needed to make his move fast.

He grabbed an unlit candle in one hand while holding the gun in the other. He tossed the candle across the room to create a diversion, then rushed straight for the figure. The red and yellow image jumped and held its hands up.

McClure switched the camera back to normal vision and the colored blur in front of him transformed into a frightened elderly man wearing a priest's collar.

"There's nothing here worth stealing, my son," said the priest.

"Who are you?" asked McClure while scanning the room for more people.

"I'm Father Nick and this is my parish. Son, you can put the gun down. I'm not going to attack you. I must admit, I've not seen a gun in years. They still scare the dickens out of me."

It was clear to McClure that this man meant him no harm and he felt a twinge of embarrassment for scaring the old guy. He put the gun in his holster. "I'm looking for a woman."

Father Nick gave him a knowing smile. "That's refreshing to hear. Please sit down and tell me more about this woman."

"Father, this young woman is in grave danger. I tracked her to this church, so if you're hiding her you need to let me know. You would be helping her, not betraying her."

"I swear to you, I am not hiding her. But, I did hear some noise in the sanctuary and I was coming to investigate when you bolted in. It's rare that I get visitors here anymore. Nowadays they have either forgotten about religion or they claim to experience their spirituality through the religious programs on Personal Vision."

McClure tried to be patient with the old man, but he knew Elizabeth was in the church somewhere. The videos showed her entering the building. As the priest spoke, McClure looked for a place where she might be hiding. There were plenty of dark areas behind pillars, under pews and even up in the choir loft.

"Excuse me, Father, but there's a really bad guy searching for this same woman and I need to locate her quickly."

Father Nick pointed to the back of the church. "Would that be the really bad guy?"

A figure stepped out of the shadows. "Hello, McClure. I was waiting for you to find Elizabeth for me, but it seems like you've been busy chit-chatting. Go ahead and keep on talking while I have a look around."

McClure shouted, "Stop right there," and raised his gun.

"Wow, look at that antique. I doubt it still works," the man said.

McClure shot the hand off a statue next him.

The man stepped behind a column.

"That's St. Peter," Father Nick said in horror. "Please, this is a house of worship, no shooting."

"Next time it will be you that I hit, so I suggest give yourself up," barked McClure.

McClure noticed the man's eyes scanning the sanctuary as if trying to pick up on the subtlest sounds or movement. As the intruder looked around, McClure grabbed a snapshot of him in his mind and sent it into the central criminal database for a crosscheck. Within seconds he had a match. Al Delaney. According to his files, he had been incarcerated for aggravated assault. In court he had been given the choice to voluntarily implant Personal Vision in order to receive constant anger management therapy and be released on probation or to serve a year in prison. He'd chosen prison.

"Okay, McClure," Al said. "You got me. I'm going to stay right here." He released a drone. It hovered a few feet in the air above him and then moved towards the confessionals.

McClure took a shot and the remnants clanged to the stone floor.

"Lucky shot, McClure."

"Al, lie face down on the ground with your arms outstretched," McClure demanded.

Al cocked his head. "Huh, that Personal Vision can come in handy sometimes."

McClure wished he had back up, but he'd promised Mr. Jenkins that he would do this on his own. The boss didn't want anyone else to know what was happening, even with his own daughter in danger. McClure hadn't worried that his earlier search of the criminal database would set off any internal alarms at HQ because the system was used thousands of times per day.

Suddenly, McClure noticed movement in the doorway. Someone else had entered the church.

"Come into the light so I can see you," McClure said.

His partner, Goodwin, emerged from the darkness with one hand up. McClure breathed a sigh of relief. "Goodwin, how did you know I was here? Cuff the man. I have you covered."

Instead, Goodwin pointed a controller at him.

"Sorry, partner," he said. "The pain was too much. This is the only way to make it stop."

McClure noticed a scab forming around the opening of Goodwin's PED.

The vibrations in McClure's head were mild at first, but they quickly increased in intensity and froze all his muscles. The gun fell from his hand and he collapsed to the floor.

Thirteen

ELIZABETH HEARD WHAT sounded like a solid object hit the cement floor followed by a groan of pain. She tucked herself further into the corner of the confessional. She thought about helping the agent, but she knew it would be useless. She knew that as soon as she stepped out, the debilitating signals would bombard her again and she, too, would be a motionless lump on the ground.

"Elizabeth, I know you're in here," Al said. "Agent McClure is going to suffer until you come out. We won't hurt you. Mr. Goodwin and I will just take you back to Socratease and we'll finish what we started."

She knew it was risky, but she had to look out from her hiding place to see what was happening. Higher up in the confessional door was a very small metal mesh opening. She edged her way up until she had a partially clear view of the sanctuary. In the middle of the sanctuary she spotted the man with the foul breath who had been pursuing her.

"There is no one else here," Father Nick said. "Please leave."

Al turned to Goodwin, "Adjust it to the seizure setting."

Goodwin hesitated and swallowed.

"Come on, Goodwin," Al challenged. "We both know you don't have a spine. You barely had the new chip in your head this morning before you started crying for mercy and telling me everything about your partner, McClure. If you delay one more moment, you'll be on your knees again, begging for the pain to stop."

Father Nick slowly maneuvered himself between Goodwin and McClure. He held up a hand. "This man doesn't deserve what you're doing."

With an angry sneer, Al turned to the priest. "You, of all people, should appreciate what we're doing. Look at this dark, empty place. At one time, this was filled every Sunday. They don't need you or your God anymore. They don't need their friends or family. All they think they need is beamed into their minds. But what they don't know is that it's killing them. Either their fragile minds can't handle the overstimulation or they escape into their fantasies and wither away. Father, we're on a mission. We're going to shut it all down and the girl that you're hiding is the key. Her father is responsible for so much misery and so many deaths."

"I swear to you, I don't know of anyone hiding here."

Al grabbed the controller from Goodwin and pressed a button. McClure began convulsing on the floor. The back of his head repeatedly hitting the cold, hard ground.

Father Nick knelt next to him and placed his hand under McClure's head to cushion the blows. "This is not the way. This man has done nothing to you."

Elizabeth heard McClure struggling for breath. It sounded as if he were choking on his tongue.

"That's enough," said Goodwin.

Al punched Goodwin in the jaw. "Don't pretend to have a backbone now. You've already betrayed your partner because you can't take a little pain. I have no respect for you. All of you are weak. It's people like me who will have the power."

McClure gasped for breath. Elizabeth sensed that he would die within minutes if she didn't do something soon. She wondered if it would do any good if she gave herself up, when the intruder could take her captive and let the man die anyhow. Besides, she didn't even know him. If she stayed hidden, she could rush back to her dad for help.

She made up her mind.

Fourteen

AS SOON AS Elizabeth opened the door of the confessional and stepped out, the overpowering buzzing returned. She grabbed the back of a pew to prevent herself from falling. Through gritted teeth she yelled, "I'm here. Let him be."

With a devilish sneer, the foul breathed man turned to look at her. He pressed a button on the controller and released McClure from his torment. "Let's finish what we started before. But first, let me get rid of some trash."

He picked up McClure's gun and aimed it directly at Goodwin who was sniveling on the floor. Without hesitation, the intruder shot him between the eyes and swiveled toward McClure. "Don't worry Agent McClure, I won't kill you, yet. We have other plans for you."

* * *

McClure was too weak to move. Sweat dripped from every pore as he struggled to catch his breath. He looked toward Elizabeth who had sacrificed herself to stop his torment. The pain was subsiding in his head, but he felt guilty. He wondered if he would've done the same for her if their roles were reversed. From the corner of his eye he saw Al take something from his pocket as he knelt down next to him. Too exhausted to fight him off, McClure felt Al press the PED on the side of his head to replace his chip with the chip from his pocket.

McClure smelled flesh and metal burning as sparks filled his mind.

"I know it hurts now," Al said, "but I need you to listen to me. You will be receiving messages soon that you need to follow. If you don't, she dies. She could die many ways. Some more painful than others, so it's important that you follow the directions precisely. We'll be keeping an eye on you, so to speak."

McClure's mind felt like it was on fire as he lost his connection to the VEA databases.

All that remained was searing pain and a wisp of his own fragmented thoughts.

He could barely hear Al's distorted voice. "Father, it looks like you have a soul in need of assistance. We'll leave you here to tend to him."

Fifteen

MCCLURE SAW FATHER Nick's gentle face as he regained consciousness. Reflexively he touched the PED slot and found that a hardened scab had formed.

"How are you feeling?" Father Nick asked.

"I'm not sure yet," McClure said. "How long have I been out?"

"Not long, but that man took the young woman with him. I wanted to make sure you were okay before going for help."

Normally McClure would just visualize the code for headquarters to open a channel, but the new chip wouldn't let him. He couldn't even tap into the drones and external cameras to see if he could locate Al. For the first time in a long time, he felt helpless.

Then he heard a strange man's voice. "Hello, McClure."

He looked around the darkened sanctuary, but only saw Father Nick.

The image of a hooded figure appeared in his mind.

"McClure, this is Socratease. Welcome to a very exclusive club. You can't talk to me, but I can talk to you. I also know your every move thanks to the tracking device in the chip. It was not my intention that your partner be killed. Sometimes Al acts a bit impulsively. Believe it or not, I'm not the bad guy in this situation. Francis Jenkins and Personal Vision are the real perpetrators of evil. I now need your help to stop them."

"This is not the way to do it," McClure said aloud.

"Who are you talking to?" Father Nick asked.

"A signal from a hooded man calling himself Socratease is being sent into my head."

"Can you see anything that will give a clue as to his location?"

"No, there's just a faint pool of light around him and I can't see a background."

"We have Elizabeth and she'll be fine if you do what we say," Socratease said. "We also have another weapon to make sure you cooperate. I'll give you a taste of it right now."

A sensory overload exploded in his mind. He grit his teeth in pain. Then the signal subsided, leaving him panting in relief.

"Like I said, that is just a taste. It could get far worse if you don't listen to me. I know you're still recovering from the effects of the chip swap. I will be back in touch with you shortly with instructions. Be ready."

With his head still tingling from the surge of sound and sensation in his brain, McClure struggled to his feet. He looked around the sanctuary as if he could find an answer to his predicament. He was at an utter loss of what to do. Without the help of VEA, there was no way to track down Elizabeth's location.

Then it occurred to him.

"Father, I need a favor from you," he said. "There's a man named Orvieto where I work. I need you to send a message to him asking him to come here, but to tell no one else. He'll need his surgical kit and a hand held PED. Can you do that?"

Father Nick looked worried. "Son, I don't have a PED, so I can't send a message. There might be an old smartphone in the rectory. It's ancient, so I'm not sure it will work."

McClure had almost forgotten there was a time when two-way communication wasn't a part of the body. People lost their phones and even broke them. Personal Vision had been experimenting with surgically implanted cameras, so McClure knew the day was coming when the body and all media would become one.

"Sure, let's get it. We'll see if we can figure out how it works."

"Son, you should stay here and rest while I get it. I know that signal took a lot out of you. The girl has the same chip in her head, but she seemed okay when she hid in the confessional over there. My guess is that the metal somehow blocks the signal. You should wait there in case Socratease tries to reach you again. I'll be back in a moment."

Sixteen

FRANCIS JENKINS SAT at his desk in the middle of his sterile office. No artwork or personal mementos decorated the walls or shelves. Most business took place in his mind, so there was no need to pay attention to his surroundings. But now the emptiness really sunk in. He had inserted a filter chip into his PED in order to block out incoming messages. He needed time to himself. His daughter had tried to attack him and now she was probably in the hands of the saboteur Socratease.

He wondered how many others the man had infected.

His door slid open. Senator Leslie Holcomb walked in. She projected power and confidence with her perfectly coiffed silver hair and rigid demeanor.

"I wasn't expecting any visitors, Senator," he said. "I have some urgent business that I have to attend to."

Without waiting for him to offer her a seat, the senator sat in a chair in front of his desk.

"Mr. Jenkins, I would've tried to reach you via the Personal Vision communication system, but you never know who is listening in," she said. "Very few things are private these days. Are there any cameras or recording devices on in your office?"

"No, everything in this office is private."

Senator Holcomb didn't seem to believe him and scanned the room herself. "It's hard to believe there really is a place in the world without a camera picking up your every move."

Jenkins wanted her out of the room so he could figure out how to find Elizabeth or, at least, the agent he'd sent after her.

"Senator, what brings you here so late?"

"That's what I like about you, Mr. Jenkins. You get right to business. The subliminal advertising you did for me in the last election was very effective. I was elected by a wide margin in my state."

"Our power of suggestion is quite persuasive," he said proudly.

She nodded her head. "This time will be the real test, though. The former governor, a good friend of yours, might run against me. If he does, I need to know I can still count on your services."

"If you hold up your end of the bargain, the election will be yours. Personal Vision has quite a success record with the candidates it supports."

Senator Holcomb leaned in closer to his desk. "Mr. Jenkins, the vote to extend Personal Vision's government contract is coming up. There are some who complain that you have grown too powerful— that you control all information and entertainment. There is a movement afoot to diversify the market again."

Jenkins could no longer hide his irritation. "Senator, we all know what happened when there was a free market. There were too many choices and no oversight. That lack of control led to chaos and the terrorist attacks at shopping malls across the states, resulting in the death of thousands. Everything is now carefully overseen by the government and Vision Enforcement. It's in all of our best interests to maintain the status quo. We are right on the edge of internalizing cameras. No more snap-on cameras that fall off or get stolen. If you take away our contract, everything will be set back years."

"Don't pretend like everything is perfect with Personal Vision. I remember what happened in the early days. Just think if the truth got out about the surge. Mr. Jenkins, I need your word that if I vote for the extension that I have your full support even if the former governor joins the race. Do I have it?"

Jenkins stood up, straightened his suit jacket and tie and said, "Your re-election is assured. Whatever we ask the public to do for the public good, they will do. I appreciate your continued support of Personal Vision and I hope the rest of your colleagues are as wise as you are. Now, I must wish you a good night. "

She stood and nodded. "I'm glad we understand each other. You are a true patriot, Mr. Jenkins."

As she left, Jenkins replaced the chip in his PED. It was time to connect with the world again. Perhaps McClure would be calling in with an update soon. In the meantime, he sifted through the images captured by the citywide network of cameras. Perhaps, if he got lucky, he'd catch a glimpse of Elizabeth.

Seventeen

"I'D BE LYING to you if I said this won't hurt," Orvieto said jokingly while holding a micro saw in one hand.

McClure lay in the darkened confessional with his head propped up on a kneeler while Father Nick used holy water to clean the area around his PED. "Don't you have anything to kill the pain?"

"McClure, I work with dead people," Ovierto said. "They don't feel a thing when I cut them open. If you were still connected to Personal Vision, I'd just tap into that to distract you. How about if I tell you a joke?"

"Just concentrate on what you're doing and make it fast."

Orvieto let out a deep breath. "I'm just going to cut around the PED and then insert a sterile plug that I'll cauterize. That's the best I can do right now. When we have time back at the lab, I'll set you up with a new PED and you'll be right back in the system. I'll insert the corrupt chip from your skull into this hand held PED so we can view the messages Socratease is sending to you."

"Let's do it," McClure said through gritted teeth. "Don't call me a wimp if I pass out." Orvieto pressed the button and the saw jumped to life. Father Nick made the sign of the cross and said a prayer.

Eighteen

ELIZABETH COULDN'T ESCAPE her own thoughts or even control them. Random memories flashed in and out of her mind. She wasn't even sure if the memories were things she had actually experienced or were from programs she had watched.

She'd never had a dog, but she was having vivid images of a small sandy brown and black mutt named *Benji*. Whenever the dog appeared in her mind, she felt comfort, as if she were with a long lost friend. But she had no memory of spending time with the dog herself. It was as if she was watching a film.

Then the face of a beautiful, strawberry blonde haired woman filled her thoughts. She was looking right at Elizabeth with a big, warm smile. It was her mother when Elizabeth was younger, but she had trouble piecing together coherent memories and filling in the blanks of her life.

She couldn't remember spending any time together with her family. She remembered her father in his office the other day and her mother lying on the floor with her face contorted in pain, but she could not recall all three of them together and happy.

Socratease's voice filled her head. "I see you're awake."

Elizabeth returned to her surroundings. She was in a bare room with a mattress on the floor and a bottle of water and food tablets next to it. She looked up and saw a small camera in the corner.

"Where are you?" asked Elizabeth. "Show yourself."

"Not just yet. I want to leave you alone with your thoughts. Al doesn't think you're strong enough to survive without Personal Vision, but I'm hoping you'll prove him wrong. To some, the withdrawals are too great and they end up going insane or taking their own lives."

"Why are you doing this to me? What have I done to you?"

"You've done nothing, but your father has, and you are precious to him"

Elizabeth paused. She couldn't recall her father saying that he loved her, but she knew he must in his own way. He gave her whatever she wanted. "What has my father done?"

"Your father is responsible for the deaths of thousands. You've never hear about all the murders, accidents and mysterious deaths associated with Personal Vision because the Vision Enforcement hides them. Why do you think your mother is the way she is now?"

"She had a brain aneurysm," Elizabeth said.

"Is that what your father told you?" Socratease asked in a mocking tone. "I guess he didn't want you to know the truth—that he was responsible for it. There were a lot of bugs to work out when he and his crew of scientists and technicians started implanting the devices into adult volunteers. They started small with just a few channels, but as the demand for more content grew, the capacity for the brain to process the signals was strained. Then one night, there was something called the Great Surge. Have you heard of it?"

Elizabeth shook her head.

"Of course not," Socratease said. "The Personal Vision Corporation is very good at making memories disappear and persuading those in power to support it. The Great Surge was triggered by a faulty code programmed into the system that caused a huge burst of information to be broadcast all at once. The signals overwhelmed everyone with the implants. Hundreds died and others had irreversible brain damage, like your mother. To prevent that from happening again they created the removable chips that serve as filters and focus the signals into categories. That way there's a mechanism in your head that controls the stream of information being sent through the system even if there is a sudden surge."

Elizabeth was unsure what to believe. Her father never talked much about that night. Her mom had been taken away and hadn't returned for months. She eventually came home with a dead stare and couldn't move any muscles other than her eyelids and her throat to swallow. Elizabeth missed her mother terribly at first, but soon the programs being beamed into her head through the PED consumed her. Just like her mom, she'd become numb to the pain around her.

"I'll leave you to your thoughts," Socratease said, bringing her back to the present. "Enjoy your own company, because that's all you're going to have for a while."

"Why should I trust what you're saying?"

"Soon this nightmare will be over for everyone. No more mind control. Let's see if the world can handle it."

Nineteen

"THAT WILL HAVE to do for now," Orvieto said to McClure. "When I get you back to the lab later on, we'll get you a new PED. I might even be able to insert a camera in as well. We've been experimenting with cadavers and now you can be the first live patient."

McClure gingerly touched the bandage on the side of his head. "Ha, I trust you, but maybe not that much. Besides, I'm not ready for another hole in my head."

Orvieto used some wires to connect the damaged PED to a smartphone with a screen. "Man, this thing is ancient. I hope it works."

The screen was filled with digital distortion, but then an image appeared of Elizabeth sitting on the floor in an empty room.

Socratease's voice came through the speaker. "Hello, McClure. As you can see, Elizabeth is now our guest. She's in the early stages of withdrawal. Soon the lack of external stimulation will drive her mad. She'll begin talking to herself. She'll pace the room. It's really quite interesting to watch it all happen. The feebleminded go mad in just a day or so. The stronger can hold out for longer. We'll see what happens with Elizabeth. However, that could all change for her if you do as I ask. You work for her father, so he'll trust you. Meet Al inside Oak Hill cemetery in one hour. He'll have a present for you to deliver. If you don't, there are ways that I can accelerate her descent into madness. I also can make your life very painful."

A loud screeching sound emanated from the speaker as lines

vibrated across the screen. McClure let out a breath, glad the PED had been removed from his head. He remembered the paralyzing pain last time. He looked up at Father Nick and Orvieto.

"Oak Hill cemetery is on the other side of Rock Creek Park on the edge of Georgetown," he said. "He probably picked that location because there are no cameras there. We're going to have to go together, since the chip they inserted in my PED has a tracking device. They'll most likely be monitoring my movements. Once I get the package from him, I'll hand it over to you and you two can head over to Personal Vision HQ and let Jenkins know what's happening. Bring the monitor with you because they still will be watching my movements and they'll think you are me."

"What will you be doing?" asked Father Nick.

"I'll be following Al and hopefully he'll lead me to wherever they're keeping Elizabeth. Do you have another one of those smartphones?"

Father Nick thought for a moment. "I should. You know, I never throw anything away."

"Good, we'll keep in contact that way. You can let me know if Socratease appears again with any further instructions."

"What do we say to Jenkins?" asked Orvieto.

"I haven't fully figured that out yet. Did you bring your vehicle over here?"

Orvieto nodded.

"Okay, off to the cemetery."

Twenty

OAK HILL CEMETERY was founded in 1848 as a place of last repose for Washington DC's well-to-do. On its steep wooded hillside were the crypts and monuments dedicated to politicians, diplomats, businessmen, military officers and philanthropists. The ornate Victorian graves were once well cared for, but now they were in ruins. Foliage had taken over and the winding pathway was crumbling. No one visited the gravesides of loved ones anymore. Their memories were forever captured within PEDs and people could access past experiences with them as if they had just happened yesterday, the earthly remains long forgotten and left to rot.

The tall iron gates that once kept intruders out at night where twisted and broken in places, so the trio easily slipped onto the grounds.

"I'm feeling a bit handicapped here without my PED," McClure said. "Typically, I'd access the database to locate a map of the cemetery and use night vision to find my way."

"Humans survived without PEDs for thousands of years, so I think you'll be fine," Father Nick replied.

"Everyone quiet," whispered Orvieto. "It looks like we're getting another message."

"McClure," Socratease said. "I see that you've made it to the cemetery. I hope you're alone. If I find out otherwise, you'll feel my disappointment."

Father Nick looked nervously around to make sure no one was watching. "What if he sees us together? We should split up."

Orvieto held up a hand for silence. "Let's see what else he has to say."

"Follow the trail to the bottom of the hill," Socratease continued instructing. "There you will find a crypt with the name *Van Ness* carved into it. Go inside and wait for Al."

"I'll go first," McClure said. "But you guys should follow about twenty paces behind me. Socratease will be tracking my movements, but he won't be able to pinpoint me to the exact spot. Once I'm inside, keep hidden behind the crypt. I'll give you whatever Al hands me and then I'll follow him."

"Then what?" Father Nick asked.

"I'm still working on that," McClure confessed. "Fill Jenkins in and hopefully I'll be able to call you with this smartphone from the hideout and you can then send help."

Orvieto and Father Nick nodded. McClure gave a mock salute and then turned to walk down the broken path. He squinted hard to see what was in front of him. With the thick canopy of leaves over him, and very little light on the ground, he cautiously made his way.

Father Nick held onto Orvieto for guidance since he still had access to his PED and night vision.

As they descended the path, the moist air turned cooler and felt almost refreshing. There was barely a sound other than the dried leaves crunching underfoot, the croaking of tree frogs and the distant hooting of an owl. McClure's head had been filled with so many sights and sounds for so long that he had never fully focused on the sounds of nature. He'd always considered himself a moderate user of Personal Vision, but he had never turned it off before. He liked to have music playing in the background while working or exercising and to look at peaceful images after a particularly tough day. Hearing nothing but external noises made him feel vulnerable and alone as he crept towards the crypt.

He turned back to see if the others were still behind him. They were barely visible with Orvieto in the front and Father Nick clinging to him tightly. He nodded to them both and entered the open doorway. Inside his footsteps echoed in the dark void.

"Glad you could make it," Al said. He looked at the bandage on McClure's head. "Who fixed that up?"

"The priest put some ointment on my head to treat the burn left by your new chip," McClure said.

"I thought you were tougher than that."

"The priest insisted."

Al stepped into the center of the crypt where the faint light from the open doorway fell upon him. "I have the present that Socratease wants you to deliver to Jenkins."

The stench of Al's breath almost made McClure vomit. It was so pungent that he could feel it almost as much as he could smell it. McClure spoke through gritted teeth. "Why can't you deliver it yourself?"

"Come on, "Al said and laughed. "You know I'd never make it through security. But you can get right next to him. Use this specially calibrated controller to paralyze him and then replace his chip with this one."

Al pressed both objects into McClure's hands. "His daughter failed, but I have more confidence in you."

"Then what?" asked McClure.

"You don't need to know everything right now. Just do as we say and we'll let Elizabeth go. It will be a different world after that. Now get out of here. We'll know when the job is done."

McClure stepped out of the crypt and walked around behind it. He silently handed the controller and the chip over to Orvieto and then motioned for him to leave. As Orvieto and Father Nick gingerly made their way back up the hill, McClure hid in the shadows and waited for Al to emerge.

Seconds gave way to minutes, but Al didn't come out. McClure looked around to see if he had somehow sneaked out unnoticed, but saw no signs of him. Finally, McClure decided to risk a look inside. He edged his way back to the doorway, peered through, but saw nothing. Then, suddenly, a fist hit his bandaged temple.

Twenty-One

MCCLURE BROUGHT HIS left arm up to block the next punch. Then, with his right, he landed an uppercut to Al's gut. Surely Al had stayed hidden to make sure that he wouldn't be followed and it had worked. McClure's impatience had given himself away.

Al bent over from the punch to the stomach, and McClure bloodied his nose with a left hook. He wasn't going to let Al beat him again.

Before Al could shake it off, McClure grabbed him by the throat and shoved him against the stone wall. Al tried desperately to break his grip, but McClure held firm. He could feel Al struggling for breath.

Al's eyes bulged and a gurgling sound came from his mouth before he went limp. McClure released his grip and let Al slide to the floor.

As McClure felt for a pulse on Al's neck, Al sprung to life and kicked him squarely in the gut.

McClure staggered back, trying to catch his balance, as Al stood and launched himself at him.

McClure couldn't move fast enough. Al slammed him into the wall. He elbowed the small of Al's back, but to no effect.

"I'm getting really tired of you, Agent McClure. I don't care if Socratease wants you alive. I'm going to finish you now."

"And I've had more than enough of you," McClure returned, elbowing Al in the back again.

Al let go.

The two faced each other in the near darkness. McClure felt blood trickling down the side of his head from where the PED had been removed. Al's face was a bloody mess, his nose twisted to one side.

Al feigned an attack, but McClure jabbed him in the face. Al screamed in pain and in a blind rage threw himself at McClure. McClure dodged to the side and swept his leg under Al's feet. Al fell forward and McClure heard his skull crack on the marble altar in the back of the crypt.

Al collapsed to the floor. His eyes staring blankly as blood pooled around his head. This time, McClure knew. Al was not getting back up.

Twenty-Two

JENKINS CONNECTED HIS mind to the municipal surveillance system. He visualized Elizabeth's face and ran a facial recognition program to see if any cameras had picked her up recently. He saw her enter the church, followed by McClure and Al—and finally Goodwin.

He fast-forwarded until he saw Al leaving the church with Elizabeth. Al looked around, spotted the camera and then disabled it with some kind of disruption device as he forced Elizabeth into a car. Camera feeds along the vehicle's path were also disabled.

Jenkins pounded his fist on the table.

He'd lost his wife with the early generations of Personal Vision and now he might lose his daughter.

He also risked losing his government supporters and his government contract. There were a lot of potential competitors out there, and competition was not a good thing. Monitoring and regulating all the signals was extraordinarily difficult. The antigovernment militia groups had taken advantage of that freedom. By hacking into a network with unsophisticated defenses, they were able to easily control the weak-minded who carried out those horrible atrocities in those series of terrorist attacks years earlier.

Now the man calling himself Socratease was trying to use his own daughter to bring down everything he had built.

Suddenly an incessant beeping in his mind interrupted his thoughts. Someone was using the emergency frequency that bypasses the chip filters.

"Yes?" he asked, using his thoughts.

"Excuse me, sir," a security officer said in a serious voice. "One of our medical examiners, Jim Orvieto, says he needs to see you. He's with a priest and he says it involves your daughter."

"Send them up," Jenkins said.

Elizabeth had hidden in a church. The priest must have seen her.

Twenty-Three

ELIZABETH HAD NEVER paid much attention to her breathing before. She just took it for granted. Now, when she concentrated, she could even hear the whoosh of blood pumping through her ear canals.

The new sensory experiences overwhelmed her and she felt panic rising inside her, but she was determined not to give in. She listened to her breath again. In and then out. In and out. Concentrating on her breathing brought her calm. It gave her something to focus on. It was something that she could control.

* * *

Socratease watched Elizabeth on the monitor with frustration. Others had broken much faster. Without the mental escape and distraction of Personal Vision, he'd seen other people struggle with their sensory withdrawals for hours, and even days, before they eventually became accustomed to their new reality. They'd pace the room, rock back and forth or cry out for relief. For a moment, he thought she was going to be like the rest, but this wasn't the case. He hadn't expected such mental toughness. He needed her in an agitated state. It was time to take her down memory lane.

* * *

Socratease disrupted her trance-like state.

"Rest time over. I'm going to send you a memory stored in the chip we took from you."

"How do you have my memories?"

"This was not intended by your father, but the brain and the electronic devices actively exchange information. So much so that you sometimes confuse memories with movies, videos or news pieces. But your real memories are stored in the chips. I've searched yours and found some interesting things you may have forgotten about. Like this."

Elizabeth saw a child's hand outstretched in front of her. It looked like her hand. It was filled with blood. She was rushing down a hallway and pushing open a door. A bedside lamp turned on in a dark room. A woman with a freckled face and strawberry blonde hair looked at her with concern.

Her mother.

"Honey, what happened to you?" she asked.

"My nose is bleeding," a young Elizabeth said, sobbing.

Her mother picked her up and held her tightly in her arms. "I know exactly what to do. That used to happen to me when I was your age. You'll be okay, honey. I promise."

Elizabeth felt warm, safe and loved.

"That was your mother," Socratease said. "A nice woman. I wish I had had a mother like that. But then yours wasn't like that for much longer."

A new memory flooded Elizabeth's mind. Again, she was running down the hall, but this time when she opened the door she saw her mother convulsing on the floor, her eyes open wide in panic. Elizabeth saw the PED in her mother's temple. The slot wasn't there in her previous memory.

"Your mother's mind is gone," Socratease said. "She's now just a shell of a person. I know it's awful, but believe me, worse has happened because of Personal Vision. The system was imperfect at first. Surges of information damaged brain cells. Your mother was one of the early victims, but your father covered it up. If people found out the true dangers of Personal Vision his work would be shut down. Your father didn't care about what he did to your mother or what could happen to you once the device was implanted. All he cared about was the power this device could give him once he perfected it. He would be able to control minds. There are more memories I want to share with you. You'll be a changed person."

Twenty-Four

THE PHONE IN McClure's pocket vibrated and rang with a church bell ring tone. He held it in front of him, unsure what exactly to do with it. He put it in front of his face.

"Hello?"

It kept ringing. He examined the sides for buttons, but the only ones he found changed the volume. He recalled seeing an old show with this device. He swiped the screen with his finger and the bell chimes finally stopped.

"McClure, you there?" Orvieto asked through the tiny speaker.

Cautiously putting the phone next to his ear McClure said, "I'm still in the cemetery. Are you with Jenkins?"

"Yeah, we're in his office. We just received the message that Socratease sent you. We can see Elizabeth in what looks like a cell. She's sobbing into her hands. It's shaken up Jenkins pretty bad."

"Any clues as to where she is?"

"We do have a clue. Al used a disrupter signal to hide his getaway from the church. It caused all the cameras within a certain radius to lose their transmission signals so that we couldn't see him. However, I programmed the system to trace the path of disruption. It goes up to Northwest DC where the old local TV stations used to be."

McClure felt buoyed. "That's great. You've got him. Is Jenkins sending in the VEA team to get the son of a bitch?"

Ovierto hesitated. "Jenkins is refusing. He wants to go with us, but

79

with no one else. I think he doesn't want to draw attention to Personal Vision. His contract is up for renewal with Congress and this could threaten that and cause some doubt. At least, that's what I suspect."

"The man is an idiot. This is his daughter's life we're talking about."

"You can tell him that when we pick you up. I'm sure Socratease thinks you're with Jenkins now thanks to the tracker in the chip. He's expecting you to bring him Jenkins…alone. We'll meet you at the zoo entrance on Connecticut Avenue. See you soon."

Orvieto's voice was gone. McClure shook his head. The Vision Enforcement Agency was created just for cases like this one. Jenkins should use all of his power to shut this madman down before he does too much damage.

He had to move, but without a visual connection to a night vision camera, McClure struggled to see in front of him. He could barely make out a path at the bottom of the hill. He'd jogged it before, but in the daylight. It was the trail at the bottom of the Rock Creek Park stream valley. If he followed it up, it would lead to the lower part of the National Zoo. From there he could make his way up the hill to Connecticut Avenue.

After stumbling through the underbrush, McClure's feet connected with solid ground. He was on the path. As he picked up his pace, he noticed how quiet the park was. There was no music in his head to distract him. He heard crickets chirping, then a soft hoot. An owl. He'd seen them on programs, but never in person.

He reached the small bridge spanning the creek that led to the zoo's empty parking lot. The zoo had been shut down long ago. Most of the animals had been either quietly euthanized or, according to rumors, released into the park.

McClure had just made his way past what used to be Lion and Tiger Hill and approached the ape house when he heard something in the bushes to his left. Startled, he jumped to one side.

An unkempt man with wild eyes staggered out of the foliage toward him. "Do you have a chip you can spare?"

McClure shook his head and turned to continue his run, but another large figure blocked his way. It was a foul-smelling PEDhead. The man gave him a menacing stare. McClure saw people coming toward him from all directions. He'd stumbled into a PEDhead homeless camp.

The first man spoke again. "Give us whatever you have. We share everything we get."

McClure pulled off his bandage to reveal the wound on the side of his head. "There's nothing to take."

"Come on, you look like a VEA agent," the first man said and sneered. "You always carry spare chips. If you don't give them to us, we'll take them from you." The group closed in.

None looked strong to McClure, but they had numbers on their side. He could grab one and twist his elbow joint so he would scream out in pain and perhaps frighten the others away, but he had become accustomed to using the controller and was out of practice.

And anyway, the man was right. VEA agents did carry spare chips. They were geared toward work and had limited entertainment value, but these PEDheads didn't know that. He reached for the pouch on his belt and pulled a few out. He held them up so everyone could see them.

The first man lunged, but McClure moved them out of his reach. "If you want them, then get them," he said and threw them in the opposite direction. The PEDheads converged on the chips and fought over them. McClure ran up the hill as fast as he could. He turned back and looked at the melee he had created. A mass of humans was fighting over the chips like starving people thrown a loaf of bread.

He was now on a meandering path led to the elephant house. As McClure ran past it, he saw shadows moving in the entryway. *More PEDheads?* If so, they wouldn't be able to catch up with him. He continued uphill. Then he heard growls.

Twenty-Five

ELIZABETH SLUMPED ON the floor and tried to control her sobbing. Emotions that she had not experienced since childhood overwhelmed her. Not until recently did she want to connect physically and emotionally with others. It took her a while to realize that it was what she'd wanted when she'd been drawn to public places like the dance club. She'd never engaged in direct conversation with strangers, but she liked being near them and sharing experiences. Her curiosity had brought her here, to this place. Maybe, she thought, she should have kept to herself. That, perhaps, would've been safer.

The sound of the door opening snapped her out of her thoughts. A hooded Socratease made his way into the room slowly. She struggled to compose herself. She felt vulnerable in front of him and she didn't like letting him feel that he had power over her. She shook her head to clear her mind and stood up in a defiant pose.

"It's about time we met face to face," she said as bravely as possible.

"Your father will be here soon and we need to get ready for him. My preference is that he does what I ask willingly. That's where I will need your help. If he resists, I'm afraid things won't be very pleasant for you. I still can send very painful signals into your mind and no parent, no matter how neglectful, wants to see their child suffer."

"Does this give you some sort of pleasure?" asked Elizabeth.

"Nope, no pleasure. I am just trying to put a stop to something that is killing people and killing society itself."

"Why does it matter to you?"

Socratease pulled back his hood and with sad eyes, looked down at Elizabeth. "Because Personal Vision made me kill my family."

Twenty-Six

MCCLURE WASN'T SURE if he should run or back away slowly. If he ran he might trigger a chase response in whatever it was in the elephant house. But if he didn't move, the creature might be on him in seconds. He wished he could tap into night vision.

The growling became louder. There was more than just one of the creatures in the doorway. He could make out shadows now. He saw four darkened figures inching their way out into the open. When the moonlight hit them, he could see clearly that they were wolves or wolf-dog hybrids.

They stared intently at him with their teeth bared. With the fur up on their backs, they looked large and intimidating. McClure searched for something he could use as a weapon. The closest thing to him was an abandoned enclosed popcorn booth. If he could make it inside, perhaps he could be safe until help arrived.

He backed up slowly without taking his eyes off the approaching predators. Two of the wolves fanned out to either side, leaving two in the middle, so they could encircle him. McClure needed to move quickly before his path to the booth was cut off. Perhaps if he bluffed, he could buy himself some time.

He puffed himself up and let out a loud guttural yell. The big wolf in the center paused and cocked his head. Time to run. McClure made a break for it.

The wolves chased him. The popcorn booth was only a few feet away, but McClure heard claws scraping cement as they gained on him. He imagined their teeth digging into his flesh. The door was right in front of him. He grabbed it, turned the knob and pulled, but it didn't budge. He turned to face the wolves and heard something whir past him.

It thudded into the wolf closest to him. It yelped in pain and surprise. McClure could see it now. It was somebody's personal drone. It circled around the wolf and then crashed into the head of another one. The wounded animal jumped back and made a dash for the elephant house. Two of the other wolves followed, but the leader remained, as if trying to decide whether or not a meal was worth the fight. The drone slammed into the back of its head and knocked it to the ground.

Dazed, it struggled to its feet and slowly made its way back to the enclosure.

McClure looked at the drone that now hovered in front of his face. He smiled and gave a friendly salute. "Whoever you are, you saved my ass."

"Thank me later," Orvieto said in the distance. "I don't want to become dog food, so let's get the hell out of here. The car is up at the Connecticut Avenue entrance."

Twenty-Seven

WHEN MCCLURE SLID into the back seat of the vehicle, Father Nick patted his shoulder in relief. McClure flinched as if he'd been slapped.

He had not been touched in a long time except during physical confrontations with suspects. And he couldn't remember anyone touching him gently since his father had laid his hand on his shoulder at his younger brother's funeral. His mother sobbed in a chair, but no one consoled her. He was ten at the time and his brother was two. Like most two year-olds, his brother had been rambunctious and required constant vigilance. Still, he had fallen off the second-floor landing of their home and broke his neck. Their mom had been upstairs with him, but hadn't been paying attention. Entertainment implants hadn't been invented yet. His mother just needed a break with an immersion visor. She later told investigators that she thought her son had been napping and that she had only escaped for a moment.

McClure's father never forgave her for what she called a *brief indulgence*. He'd lectured her many times about the visor and had threatened to destroy it on multiple occasions. She'd promised to cut back, but she felt drawn to it. McClure had vowed to use Personal Vision in moderation when it was finally introduced, having witnessed the pain it had caused his family.

"Are you okay?" asked Father Nick. "I didn't mean to startle you."

McClure shrugged. "No, don't worry. I'm just a bit on edge. I'm sure glad to see you guys. There's more help coming, right?"

Everyone in the vehicle looked to Jenkins in the front seat. He gave them a solemn look in return. "We know exactly where this guy is located and we don't need to attract a lot of attention."

McClure shook his head. "He has your daughter. Let's call in the Rapid Response Team. This is exactly what they are trained for."

Jenkins gave him an icy stare. "Believe me, I know what's at stake. The more people we involve in this, the more chances that something will go wrong."

"With the greatest respect, sir, I'm afraid I have to disagree. Our best chance is to go in there quickly with superior force."

"At this point, I'm not sure who to trust. Look what happened to your partner, Agent McClure. Who knows who else has been corrupted at this point."

The vehicle moved silently and quickly up Wisconsin Avenue. McClure felt sad as he looked out at the empty streetscape. At this late hour, most people were in their beds with the sleep chips in their PEDs. When they woke up, they'd change their chips, eat a food chew and go about their isolated lives. McClure wondered if Socratease's end goal was the right one. The methods were wrong, but would the end of Personal Vision really be so bad?

"What are you going to do when we confront Socratease?" asked McClure.

Jenkins stared blankly out in front of him. "He wants me and he'll get me."

"That's it?" McClure asked and scoffed. "He's not going to be satisfied with that. He wants to shut down the network and he needs you to do that. He's going to force you to act against your will. Are you ready for that?"

"He'll probably torture you with the corrupted chip," Orvieto said. "Once that gets in your head, he'll send signals into your brain that could cause permanent damage."

Jenkins blinked and turned to Orvieto. "I'm counting on him trying. You brought your field kit, right?"

Orvieto tapped the case containing his surgical tools.

"Good, you'll need to construct something for me before we get to the facility. And, McClure, your services will be required as well."

"Sounds like you do have a plan," McClure said.

* * *

Father Nick made the sign of the cross and whispered a silent prayer to himself. He didn't condone violence, but he saw what Socratease's people could do. He knew this man had to be stopped and Elizabeth saved, but hopefully without any lives lost.

This night had awoken a lot of memories in him. He hadn't felt a sense of camaraderie with other people for years. With each advancing technology, his parishioners moved farther and farther away from him. He remembered looking out at full pews as a young priest as he gave his homilies. He was a great speaker and his sermons touched a lot of lives. The church later tried to compete with Personal Vision by releasing virtual sermons, but the battle had been lost. Soon Father Nick was left with an empty, darkened church filled with only the echoes of his footsteps.

Perhaps this would be the night it all changed.

Twenty-Eight

MCCLURE FOUND A row of dead security officers in front of the former WRC-TV news studios with gunshot wounds to the head.

Jenkins stood in front of the vehicle.

"You lied to me," McClure said. "You said you weren't going to send the Rapid Response Team and yet here they are."

Jenkins was visibly shaken by what he saw. The blood on the pavement was still wet. "This didn't go as planned. I hope Elizabeth is still alive."

"Hey," Ovierto said. "Socratease is trying to communicate."

Socratease's hooded visage appeared on the monitor in Orvierto's hands. "I thought you might enjoy the welcoming committee. I know better than to trust a man like Francis Jenkins. I was ready for his hit squad. I only needed to corrupt one agent. He killed himself after killing all of his comrades. McClure, I think it's time that you learned more about your employer. I want the both of you to step inside the building. The others stay outside. You have five seconds to get in here or I send a signal to Elizabeth that she'll never forget. Now, move it."

McClure grabbed Jenkin's shirtsleeve and pulled on it. "Let's go." Jenkins resisted, so McClure jerked harder. "Look what you've done already. Let's get the hell in there."

"It could be a trap," Jenkins said.

"It probably is, but we don't have a choice."

McClure pushed him forward and they dashed for the entrance. Once inside the lobby he saw Elizabeth standing in the middle of the room with Socratease a few steps behind her pointing a controller towards her.

"Make any moves and I'll scramble her mind," Socratease said.

"Why are you doing this?" Jenkins asked. "I've done nothing to you."

Socratease pulled back his hood. McClure gasped in shock.

Standing in front of him was the man he had arrested for brutally murdering his family. His hair was receding, the wrinkles around his eyes had deepened, but there was no mistaking his identity.

"McClure, no matter what you're thinking, I am not a mad killer. I think of my family every day. I am tormented by what I did to them, but you must know that I was not in control. I used to work for the monster standing next to you. I was one of the engineers that created Personal Vision. It took a lot of trial and error to figure out how to install hardware that wasn't rejected by the body and would feed signals directly into the brain. We still had a few years of testing ahead of us before it was safe to release to the general public."

He turned to Elizabeth. "But your father had no patience for more lab testing. He convinced the engineers and other executives to release the first generation of Personal Vision. He said it was so safe that he and his wife would be among the first to have it installed."

Elizabeth glared at her father. "Is this true? You forced mom?"

"She volunteered," Jenkins said in a pleading tone. "She believed in what I was trying to do and she wanted to demonstrate her full support. I would never have forced her."

"How did this lead to you killing your family?" McClure asked.

"Everything was fine for a while when we only sent limited amounts of data through the system. We could go about our daily lives and then tune into the stream of information when we were off duty, but that wasn't enough for Jenkins. He wanted to wipe out the competition. In order to do so he wanted to offer more choices. That meant more data sent into the receivers. Soon, it became difficult to distinguish what was a memory and what was something you experienced virtually. I told my supervisors we needed a way to control the information flowing into our minds. We needed some sort of filtering system or on-off mechanism. But the answer was no. We couldn't afford to install those filters into all the PEDs yet."

"You saw what happened when there was no central control," Jenkins said. "Terrorists infiltrated the network. What we were doing was going to save lives."

"Well, it killed my family and it destroyed your wife's brain, just like it did to thousands of others. In my case, the horror movies that were streaming into my mind took over. I thought my family was possessed by evil spirits and that I had to release them from their torment." Tears streamed down Socretease's cheeks. "McClure, didn't you ever wonder what happened to me after you turned me over to VEA? You never heard of my case going to trial, right?"

McClure shook his head.

"That's because Vision Enforcement didn't want the secret out. I was taken back to their facilities where they tried to learn from their mistake. I endured countless surgeries and software upgrades while they tried to figure out how to separate memories from signals. They even tried scrubbing my mind of the entire incident."

"For what happened to your family, I am sorry," said Jenkins earnestly. "That's one of the reasons we created the chip system. It helped to safeguard against surges and overstimulation. My wife is a daily reminder to me of the horrible mistakes we made. Believe me when I say that the intention was never to hurt anyone, but only to help."

Socratease boiled with rage. "You have no idea how my family suffered. They died at the hands of the man they trusted and loved most."

He turned to Orvieto who had just entered the lobby. "Hold up that monitor in your hand so everyone can see my memories of that night. Don't turn away."

The horrid images of Socratease's wife and children running from him and pleading for their lives played out on the screen. His wife begged for mercy and asked why he was doing this. Why slay his own flesh and blood?

Tears poured down Elizabeth's face as she listened to the sounds of his children screaming out in pain and confusion.

"This plays out in my mind every day. I can't undo what I've done, but I can stop this from happening to others. Sure, you've created filters, but people no longer think for themselves. They simply accept whatever you feed them via Personal Vision and that's still dangerous. We are susceptible to foreign attack as well as self-destruction through apathy. I went through years of depression after your doctors declared me cured and released me back into society. My life lacked purpose and I was tormented by what I had done. Then I looked around me. I felt the sun on my skin, the smell of honeysuckles in the air and the touch of soft grass below my bare feet. For the first time in years, I felt connected to something. But I saw that others had stopped noticing their surroundings and the people in front of them. They were consumed by the sensations you were sending to them. People started neglecting themselves and their surroundings. Everything was decaying, but no one noticed. That's when I got my idea—use my knowledge to make them literally stop and smell the flowers. I knew where you dumped your discarded prototypes and so I started fashioning my own crude version of Personal Vision. I could not receive signals back, but I could send them out and use them to control others. My goal was to eventually get to you, and here we are."

Jenkins was almost at a loss for words. "What do you want now?"

"I want your daughter to finish what she started the other day," Socratease said.

Elizabeth gave him a puzzled look.

"That chip in your hand." Socratease said. "Put it in your father's PED."

"No," Elizabeth said.

Socratease pressed a button on his controller and Elizabeth screamed.

"Why don't you put it in yourself?" Jenkins shouted.

McClure hoped Socratease would take the bait. Orvieto had inserted a thin plastic sleeve into Jenkin's PED. It would allow the chip to slide in but would prevent contact. McClure would subdue Socratease the moment he inserted the chip.

"It means more if we keep this in the family," Socratease said.

* * *

Jenkins rushed to Elizabeth's side and held her tight. He would do anything to save her.

"If any of you make a move toward me," Socratease said. "I will increase the intensity. At the moment, whatever happens to her will be only temporary, but I could make the damage permanent."

The chip fell from Elizabeth's hand and landed on the linoleum floor. Jenkins gently laid her down and picked up the chip.

"Make it stop and I will put this in myself."

Socratease turned a dial on the controller. "I won't turn it off until you've done what you've promised, but I have lessened the power. Now do it."

Jenkins nodded faintly to McClure as a signal for him to get ready. McClure's muscles tensed. He'd rehearsed what he needed to do. While Socratease's attention was fixated on Jenkins, McClure would rush in, secure Socratease's wrist with one hand and knock the controller loose with the other. Then he'd use his knuckles to crush Socratease's windpipe.

"If I do this, do you promise to release my daughter and cease tormenting her?" Jenkins asked.

"Once you do this," Socratease said, "there will be no reason to keep her. I've tried hacking into the network to shut it down, but you've put in place too many firewalls. If I enter the system through your PED, I'll have a direct line to the heart of the beast and I will be able to release everyone."

Jenkins thought about everything he had achieved. He had

defeated all other competitors and created a single information and entertainment delivery system to the entire nation. It took years of arm-twisting, bribery and cleverness to accomplish it and now it could all be wiped out. *Was the world better off because of it?* He thought of his wife and looked down at his unconscious daughter. He thought about Socratease's wife asking *why* as she took her last breath. And he knew the answer.

"Take care of her," he said to McClure. "Let her know I always loved her and her mother."

With trembling fingers, Jenkins plied the sleeve out of the slot on the side of his head and let it drop to the ground.

Orvieto gasped. "No, there are other ways to do this. We can shut it down back at headquarters. This could kill you."

"I'm sorry," Jenkins said as he looked into Socratease's eyes. He took a deep breath and inserted the chip. He closed his eyes tight in anticipation of the pain to come, but there was nothing. Had he been spared?

The first shock hit him when he opened his eyes. He felt as if his brain were being squeezed in a vice. Sparkling colors danced in his mind amidst a cacophony of sounds and sights. A river of entertainment programs, personal messages and memories flowed through him. The surge became a flood. His last flickering sense of self was pulled into the current and washed away. He was now simply a vessel. Francis Jenkins was gone.

Twenty-Nine

SIX MONTHS LATER

THE FRECKLE-FACED five year old boy was determined not to blink. He looked intently at his older sister. If he willed himself hard enough, he knew he could win. His eyeballs were starting to dry out, and he sensed a distraction to his left, but he needed to stay focused. She had beaten him too many times in the past. He wanted to prove he had the stamina and willpower this time.

She looked right back into his eyes. Just a few more seconds and she knew he would break. Her powers of concentration were greater than his, she thought to herself. But he was holding on longer than before. She waved her hand in the air to the right in an attempt to draw his attention. He didn't react. She was in trouble. It was time to resort to a new trick. Without blinking, she said, "Quack, quack."

The boy laughed and looked away. "That's not fair," he giggled.

His sister gave him a friendly shove. "You'll never beat me at a staring contest."

"That's because you cheat."

The doctors had done a good job of removing the PED slots on their temples. The skin was slightly lighter where the gap had been, but over time, the discoloration would fade and that section would blend in with the rest of the skin. At least the young had time to heal. Older patients would carry the signs of the devices for the rest of their lives.

* * *

A few steps up from the siblings, McClure took in the sights below him. He always enjoyed the view from the Lincoln Memorial with the rectangular reflecting pool in front of him, the Washington Monument beyond and the capital in the distance. The air was clear of personal drones and the promise of spring was in the breeze. Society had survived the sudden loss of Personal Vision. It had been a struggle at first. People literally didn't know what to do with themselves. It was almost as if they had to learn to walk again. They had not exercised the muscles of face to face communication in years. Conversations were awkward and strained for a while, but soon people started gathering again. They began to laugh together and rediscover the warmth of human interaction.

Appetites were reawakened and the food chew business crashed. People rediscovered the joy of physical and sensory experiences. The smell of bacon frying, the gentle touch of a loved one and the sound of laughter. McClure was happy to be fully alive again. The one downside was that crime had gone back up again and the bad guys were in better shape, so they were harder to subdue. The VEA had closed down and McClure had lost his job, but he was quickly snatched up by the police department. They needed someone with his leadership skills to guide them through unfamiliar times.

"Time to go," Elizabeth said. "I need to study for my exam."

McClure smiled. "You'll ace it. You were born to be a teacher."

"Well, then you don't know Professor Blum. He takes no prisoners. This isn't easy, you know."

He pulled her in tight and gently kissed the top of her head. "I have confidence in you."

"I'm glad someone does," she replied. "Can we stop by and visit my parents on the way home?"

"Of course," McClure said as he traced the scar on the side of her head. He knew the visit would be short. The assisted living facility was near Georgetown, overlooking the Potomac River. Even though the setting was tranquil, it always felt a bit sad to him. All the residents had vacant looks in their eyes, so the surroundings were more for the visitors than for the occupants.

Socratease's chip had destroyed Jenkin's mind at the same time it took down the network. But McClure knew Elizabeth took comfort in the fact that her parents were together at last. She visited them each week, talked about her life and kissed them before leaving. Even though they could not respond, she had more family time with them than ever before.

* * *

The prison guard opened the door and let Father Nick into the visitor's room. Father Nick slid a metal chair up to the reinforced window. Socratease entered the room on the other side of the glass, clad in an orange jump suit. He sat down and pushed the intercom button.

"I'm surprised to see you here, Father," he said.

Father Nick chuckled. "It's not my favorite place to be. I just thought you might want someone to talk to."

Seemingly puzzled, Socratease asked, "After all that I've done?"

"Especially after all that you've done."

Socratease absently rubbed his hand through his unkempt hair. "It seems that I have a lot of time to talk now."

"I'm all ears," Father Nick said and grinned—happy to be needed.